THE NEBRASKA QUOTIENT

THE NEBRASKA QUOTIENT

William J. Reynolds

St. Martin's Press
New York

Design by Andy Carpenter

Library of Congress Catalog Number 84-51167
ISBN 0-312-56254-3

First Edition
10 9 8 7 6 5 4 3 2 1

For Peg, who daily reminds me of the possibilities

THE NEBRASKA QUOTIENT

The man with the bullet in **1** him was lucky. Ordinarily he wouldn't have found me up at 4:00 A.M. But that muggy July night I had been at the typewriter till past two, plodding away at The Book, and it had given me what the commercials like to call a nagging backache. A fitful hour or so in the sack did no good. So I got up and swallowed some little oblong capsules that Jen had left in the bathroom on her last whirlwind tour through my tiny one-bedroom apartment and my life. I was standing at the kitchen sink in my underwear and the dark, washing down the pills with cold, bitter coffee, trying to suck a breath of air through the screened windows over the sink.

That was perfectly pointless. On an Omaha summer night there isn't enough actual air in the air to inflate a kid's beach ball. There's only heat and humidity, a perpetual sauna, a gray haze through which we slog from Independence Day through Labor Day. It's a marvelous conversational icebreaker. It's also a pain. My undershirt clung to my back like steaming gauze.

I slurped at the coffee, wished my backache away and listened to the traffic on the Radial whispering like lovers in the hot, moist darkness. The Northwest Radial Highway isn't much of a highway really, but it slices down from the extreme northwestern end of Omaha and provides a jagged but quick shot to Cuming Street. From there it's downtown, the I–80 and I–29 interchanges, then anyplace. Everyone in Omaha is on his way to anyplace. There's a lot of traffic on the Radial, even at four in the morning.

Above the incessant wavelike rolling of rubber on asphalt I heard another, sharper sound from the small living room at the front of the apartment. I half listened for that sound all summer, every summer, for all the summers I lived there. Forty-fifth and Decatur isn't the worst neighborhood in town, but it certainly isn't the best. I figured that some sultry night when I left the terrace doors open in a futile attempt to coax some circulation through the place, someone would realize that screen doors, even when locked, offer about as much resistance to a break-in as smoke. This seemed to be the night: something clumsier and heavier than the neighborhood tomcat was climbing over the aluminum rail and onto the postage-stamp-sized slab of concrete my imaginative land-lord called a terrace.

My eyes were adjusted to the dark, so I left the lights out and eased into the living room. Outside was enough of a moon to turn the sky a fuzzy, funny blue, and I could see a man, a very large man, silhouetted against that backdrop. He was making one hell of a racket getting up over the rail and onto the terrace, though it should have been an easy climb for someone his height—after all, it was only a second-floor apartment. His clumsy movements, grunting efforts and heavy breathing gave me the idea he was drunk or strung out or crazy or something.

I grabbed an electric steam iron from the board near my hip, just in case I needed a blunt instrument.

He tried the latch on the screen, found it locked, and hesitated.

Blood thudded in my ears like Clydesdales' hoofbeats. I didn't move, didn't even breathe. In the pitch-blackness of the apartment I knew I was invisible to him. That could come in handy.

Then he ripped through the screens the way wet garbage rips through a paper bag. I had my mighty iron in striking position, but I didn't need it. He wasn't breaking through the screens, he was collapsing through them, ending belly-up on the floor, where he remained, sprawled, still.

I waited: nothing. Finally I put on a light.

He lay in a tangle of ruined wire netting. I stared down at him, recognizing without pleasure the big Semitic face that went so well atop the big lumpy body. His name was Morris Copel. A little more than six years earlier he had been my partner. I hadn't seen him in that time, not since he had skipped town and left me with nothing but an empty office three months past-due on the rent.

Without setting down my iron I knelt to examine him. The summer suit he wore was old and cheap and ill-fitting. And soaking wet, as if he'd swum up the side of the building. It would take a lot of skillful pressing to put it back into anywhere near good shape. And that would be a wasted effort, because most of the left side of the coat was soaked through with sticky, shiny, red-black blood that leaked uncontrollably from his shoulder.

Besides putting a slug in him, someone with some expertise had also worked him over very conscientiously. His face—no work of art to begin with, being marred by acne scars and having a rough, lumpish look, like unsmoothed modeling clay—was a conglomeration of welts, bruises and lacerations. More than he'd've picked up going headfirst through a dozen cheap screen doors. More blood trickled from the edges of his wide, fleshy mouth than his split lip could account for. I thought he was surely dead. But the lead-colored eyes staring blankly at my ceiling registered when I crossed their field of focus. Copel worked his wrecked lips. A week or so later he managed my name:

"Nebraska . . ."

There was a significant gurgle on the last syllable. I felt a wash of guilt for all the hatred and all the times I had wished him dead. He was nearly there now, and he wouldn't need a wish from me to help him along. "Damn you, Copel," I murmured fervently. "You've finally done it."

He hadn't done it yet, though. His right hand stirred. I hefted my impromptu weapon a little to draw attention to it, to let him know that if he pulled a shootin' iron my steam model would press his ugly face into the floorboards, regardless of his delicate condition. But instead he reached into the waistband of his sopping pants, down into his crotch, and dragged out a creased and crumpled brown letter-sized envelope, damp with humidity and the soaking he'd undergone and his perspiration and Christ knows what else. He pressed the envelope into my free fist. Then his arm fell back to the floor, as if the wire holding it had been cut. It fell hard, heavily, and something precariously balanced in the kitchen sink slipped with a *thunk*.

That *thunk*, I reflected, is the period they put at the end of your life.

Not too profound, I admit, but it was late. And the sentiment was valid enough, for with that *thunk* the selfness of him evaporated. Just like that. One minute—one second, one *fraction* of a second—a man; the next, a stiff. Looks the same, but takes on the vacant melancholy a home acquires when you close the door on it for the last time and drive away. A home becomes a house, a man becomes a stiff.

My throat was dry. I went back to the kitchen and found a bottle of root beer, cut my finger trying to unscrew the convenient unscrewable cap, swore colorfully, ripped the cap off with a pliers and fixed my drink. Sucking on an ice cube, I flipped on the fluorescent doughnut over the sink and looked at the brown envelope. I didn't care much for the thought of where it had recently been, but I couldn't fault Copel's logic: not too many men will frisk you very enthusiastically in, shall we say, the pelvic region. That Copel kept his little envelope through all he'd obviously gone through was sufficient proof of that.

The envelope was unmarked and unsealed, but dampness caused the flap to stick unevenly. I peeled it back and slipped out the contents: four strips of color negatives, four frames per strip, and two larger unmounted color transparencies, all glued together by humidity. I separated them and, in succession, held them to the light.

They were of a woman. She was young—late twenties, early thirties—nice-looking and blond. Blond all over. They were that sort of pictures. Feeling a lot like a 37-year-old dirty old man, I rummaged for and found an ancient chipped magnifying glass with which to study them.

From a technical standpoint they were awful—and that's being kind. They were amateurish nudie shots is all, harshly lighted with a flash rather than a spotlamp, snapped in somebody's living room rather than a studio. Hopelessly inept. I turned my attention to the blonde.

She wore only high heels and a worried expression. She displayed herself. She writhed on thick carpeting—blue, if you care—in what was probably not passion. She bent over, facing away from the lens, adjusting the strap of one shoe. Eyes closed, she caressed herself disingenuously. She exhibited herself in a lackluster fashion more pathetic than erotic. And the invading eye of the camera observed, unsympathetically, and recorded.

Posing hadn't been the blonde's idea. While she was beautiful enough for it—small-breasted, long-limbed, golden—she made no attempt at simulating the abandon, the idyllic postures affected by the girls in the slick men's magazines. That was evidence enough of her unwillingness, I thought, but there was more—there was the look in her eyes, a look very much like the scared, sharp gaze of wild animals caught at night, surprised in the white glare of automatic flash cameras. Everything about the pictures suggested that the blonde was afraid *not* to appear in them, and that made them all the more repulsive—or, I suppose, titillating, depending on your persuasions.

And these even had an extra measure of degradation that I was certain increased their market value: the image of a man. He didn't participate; he merely stood, fully clothed, his back to the camera, in each of the frames. Watching what the woman did—or forcing her, by his presence, to do it?—robbing her of any pretension to artistry, making her naked rather than nude, making her an object.

These were dirty pictures in any number of senses.

I studied the woman's face carefully, trying to decode the psychedelic wash of jumbled colors, then, reluctantly, checked the unmounted slides. I was afraid of that: I knew her.

Rather, I recognized her, knew her only slightly and from long ago. Her name was Adrian Mallory, and she was the daughter of the Honorable Daniel G. Mallory, senior U.S. senator from the state of Nebraska. I had worked for Mallory briefly, back when I was but a callow political science student at Omaha U., now the University of Nebraska at Omaha. That was some eighteen years ago, when state senator Mallory had decided the political climate was conducive to taking his liberal ideas from the unicameral, where they were in danger of dying from loneliness, to a national setting. He was right. Though the state is, or is thought of as, a typical Midwestern conservative stronghold, Mallory was saying all the sorts of things that people—particularly young, idealistic people like me—wanted to hear in the early 1960s. Better, he was shrewd enough to get in and shrewd enough to stay in even when the political winds shifted, as they had. Now standing for his fourth term, Mallory was considered only a slight favorite: the New Right or somebody had "targeted" him for defeat that year. It was shaping up to be a tough campaign, but so was his first.

I knew Adrian Mallory because my role on Mallory's staff during that first race pretty much boiled down to keeping her name out of the press. That was a full-time job. Left to herself, the little monster would've been in the news more than her old man. She was forever getting picked up on a liquor violation, swiping something worthless out of a Ben Franklin's, taking off for Mexico with a bubbleheaded boyfriend and getting about as far as Lincoln, setting fire to a schoolmate's locker or some damn other thing. I didn't much like the job of picking up after her, of sweet-talking shop owners and principals and harried cops into chalking it up to youthful exuberance. But I liked Mallory and what he represented, so when he took me down to the corner and bought me a couple beers and told me how tough it was for poor little Adrian, growing up without a mommy and hardly a daddy, and said he'd consider it a personal favor if I'd do what I could to see they didn't work the poor sweet baby over too badly—well, you get the picture. I bought it like a used car, put up with it until Mallory was safely elected, then cut out and made it somebody else's headache. And a headache it surely was for that somebody, thanks to Adrian's uncanny knack for acquiring the wrong sort of friends.

I hadn't seen her in eleven or twelve years and hadn't even heard about her for four or five, but it looked like she hadn't lost the knack.

It also looked like I had more in my hand than dirty pictures. Dan Mallory was an important man in the party, a standard-bearer, as they say, and there was some talk of standing him for vice president the next time out. How many points in his career would be better made for blackmail?

I wiped the pictures dry, put them back in their envelope, put the envelope under the Rubbermaid cutlery tray in a drawer in the sink cabinet. Then I went back to the living room to see if Copel was comfortable.

He was about as comfortable as you get. I searched him and came up with the usual assortment of stuff, including a phonied P.I.'s permit and an expired Conoco card. Nothing else, except damp lint. Whatever brought him to me, whatever he was involved in, whatever he might have had to say would go unsaid—unless the woman in his pictures, however they entered into things, was talkative. As I hoped she'd be: although I was trying hard to make my living as a free-lance writer, the magazines hadn't been over-whelmingly generous lately. I had a few checks "in the mail," as the litany goes, but in the meantime I figured it was a good idea to swallow the principles that said I was now a writer, no longer a private investigator, and see if Adrian Mallory could be convinced that she needed my incomparable professional services. With the end of the month approaching, I knew my landlord would appreci-ate the effort.

But first there was the little matter of the corpse in my living room, and the Omaha Police Division.

OPD is, by and large, made up of a pretty good sort of cop in a city just big enough to be bitchy, a city with more than its share, per capita, of the kinds of inhabitants that Chambers of Commerce don't brag about. I'd been a private detective, a newspaper re-porter, a security cop and a few other things in Omaha, and I never had too much trouble with OPD, even when I wouldn't blame them for giving me some. Still, you've got to expect even the most easygoing of cops to have a question or two to bounce your way when you call at 4:30 in the morning to have them come collect a body from your living room floor. In fact, under those circum-stances, things can get pretty uncomfortable for you pretty fast. Fortunately, it turned out that I knew the homicide detective in charge fairly well, from the old days.

His name was Ben Oberon, he was maybe forty-five years old

and he comported himself gingerly, as if perpetually afraid you were going to try to sell him something. Lieutenant Oberon was tall and thin—skinny, more accurately—but his skin was curiously loose and baggy, fitting him about as well as his clothes usually did. Tonight he wore a gray three-piece number that he must have been melting in. The point of his tie peeked from below his lowest vest-button.

We shook hands.

"It's been a while," said Oberon. "I was a little surprised when the call came in, in fact. I thought I'd heard you're out of the business."

"More or less. But in this case I'm strictly the innocent by-stander." I pointed with my chin at the body on the floor not four feet from us. "Remember him?"

Oberon went over and knelt near Copel. At about that time the coroner's people started infiltrating the cramped room. I imagined the mercury climbing another quarter-inch or more.

"Not pretty," Oberon said blandly. "Your partner, isn't he? Now, what was that name?—Cohen? Coppel?"

"Copel. Morris. And he was my partner—with emphasis on the 'was.'"

Oberon's fingers tested the dampness of Copel's lapels, as if he were thinking of buying the suit, but his face was aimed at me. His eyebrows went up and his mouth went down, bracketed by flabby parentheses, but he said only, "Yeah?"

"Yeah." I explained the bit: that I knew Copel slightly when we were both rent-a-cops with Greater Omaha Security Service. That he seemed all right, so I listened when he started talking about wanting to set up a little agency of his own. I was looking for something else, too, and while neither of us alone had enough of a bankroll to do anything, together we could just about swing it.

The catch was, Copel had come into his bankroll by dint of some rather foolhardy arrangements with local representatives of the Cosa Nostra. "First thing you know," I told Oberon, "I come to the office one morning to find that everything except the roaches in the john has been cleared out. Presumably in lieu of payments on something. Copel's gone too."

Oberon pulled a sympathetic face.

"He blew on out of town then—I know because I looked for him for a couple months, with an eye toward putting him in just about the shape you see him now. But with no money coming in, and bills yet to pay on the reclaimed furniture, I had to involve myself in more profitable ventures. They say revenge is sweet; all I ever learned was that it's damned expensive. I went solo then, and ever since I've either worked for myself or jobbed out to agencies. Of course, I make most of my living now as a writer—chiefly magazine articles." I didn't say anything about The Book. I tend not to talk about The Book, my great work of detective literature that was going to put my name up there with Hammett, Chandler and Macdonald. And, not incidentally, make my fortune. I thought about it a lot, daydreamed about it a lot, worked on it when I could steal the time, but kept pretty closemouthed about it. Would-be writers spend too much time emoting about their would-be writing.

"And that's the last you saw of him?" Oberon prompted.

"Till tonight, of course. That makes it just over six years—which was your next question, right?"

Oberon grinned a little. "Maybe something like that."

"Thought so. I watch all the cops-and-robbers shows, you know. Anyway, that's just about how he showed up. I'm amazed he even made it over the railing—he could hardly stand up, as you've probably gathered from the condition of those screens. My landlord's gonna love this."

"Tell him it was big moths." Oberon turned his large, sad, liquid eyes in the direction of the ruined patio doors, nodding slightly to himself, as if making mental notes on another subject altogether. After another look at the dead man, he rose and wandered the short distance to the doors, looked out into the night and then back at me. "So what's the story?" he wondered aloud after thinking about it a while.

Moisture had collected on Oberon's top lip, and I found myself reflexively wiping my own mouth before I answered. "I heard a noise on the patio. I'd had trouble sleeping so I was up and out in the kitchen. I came over to investigate."

"And this was . . .?"

"A couple minutes past four."

He wrote it down. "'Kay."

"Someone was coming over that rail there. I always worry about that when I have the glass doors open, like I did tonight, to try to get some breeze through here."

"Good luck."

"Tell me. Anyhow, you can see that anyone of reasonable height can hop up onto the railing around the patio of the apartment downstairs and hoist himself onto mine. Which is what he was doing, though of course I didn't know who he was yet; all I could see of him was a silhouette. He fiddled with the latch some, and then hit on the clever idea of poking a hole in the screens with his head. Only he strained himself too much so he had to lie down on the floor and rest."

The moist eyes fixed on me. "How'd he get wet?"

"He came that way. At first I thought he'd taken a dip in my private pool, but I notice it's been drained."

Oberon looked at me like he was going to ask what rock I'd come from under. Contritely, I said, "In weather like this people leave their yard sprinklers on all night. Copel was trying to get away from whoever did this to him; he could have stumbled through a sprinkler somewhere."

"It's kind of miraculous he was even able to get up here, isn't it?" Oberon said musingly, half to himself. Then, before I could compose a witty rejoinder, "Any idea who roughed him up?"

"Not the slightest." The police photographer's flash exploded then and sliced through the room like heat lightning across the Midwestern sky, reminding me, guiltily, of the pictures Copel had carried—the negatives and slides that the detectives carefully removing and cataloguing his effects wouldn't find. I didn't like misleading Oberon and his men, didn't like withholding evidence, or potential evidence. After all, they were just guys, just trying to get their jobs done. But I knew that those pictures, once in OPD's mitts, were as good as in the public domain. While I couldn't deny my profit motive in the matter, I also thought I'd give Adrian Mallory a break, if only for her father's sake.

That didn't make lying to Oberon any easier. I liked Oberon.

He'd always been more than straight with me. I wanted to be up-front with him now. "He started to say something but he didn't get past my name," I volunteered limply. So much for up-frontness.

Oberon looked up briefly, then back down to the silent body and the men who labored over it. "Why do you suppose he came to see you? I mean, with everything and after so much time . . ."

"I wonder. I didn't spend much time thinking he'd come to settle up because his conscience'd been bothering him all these years. So I figure he must've been in big trouble—pretty obvious, I guess—and managed to get away from whoever put him in big trouble. Probably not far from here, this was, because he couldn't've gone far in that condition. He must've remembered I lived around here, and decided to try his luck and see if I'd hide him."

"Who from? The mob?"

"He did have a history of sort of rubbing them the wrong way from time to time."

"Yes he did. Then I suppose that's how we'll have to approach it until we know otherwise." He trained a suspicious eye on me. "Meantime, I'm not going to have any trouble with you, am I?"

"I'll be around town," I said.

"What I mean is, I'd rather not have you poking your nose into this, gumming up me and my men."

I gave him a look. "You have me confused with Sam Spade. My devotion to a partner—especially *that* partner—just doesn't run that deep." Oberon started to speak. I cut him off. "Look, in the first place I'm not that interested in who killed Copel. Un-charitable, but true. He was a small-timer with the bad habit of trying to cross big-timers, and I figure he just did it once too often. Good riddance, as the saying goes."

Oberon studied my features as if memorizing them. I stared back, the very picture of innocence, trying not to think about all I was holding back from him.

"And in the second place?" he said, catching me off guard.

"Say what?"

"You said that in the first place you had no interest in knowing who killed Copel. That implies a second place."

"Yes it does. And a third place, in fact. In the second place,

I'm trying to make my living as a writer. I go back to the old business only when I'm forced to—I certainly don't go out of my way looking for busywork when I don't need the money.

"And that brings us to the third place: you know as well as I do that it's bad policy—and damned expensive, besides—to take on a case without a client to foot the bills." I spread my arms. "I certainly don't see anyone busting in the door to hire me to find Copel's killer, Ben, do you?"

Oberon gave me a distracted, narrow smile. It could have meant anything, or nothing. I smiled back and went on trying not to think of the penalties for withholding evidence in a homicide.

For the second time that **2** night/morning I couldn't sleep. It was almost full light by the time I got rid of the cops, the coroner and a nightside metro reporter for the *World-Herald*, and though my body had had it, my keyed-up brain, whizzing like a perpetual-motion machine stuck in high gear, tried vainly to make sense of the equation it had only a couple of variables to. The desire to have everything fit together like pieces of a well-made puzzle is an occupational hazard shared by writers and detectives alike. After some fifteen years building stories or cases, trying to make sense of *everything* is second nature. It gives me trouble when I'm faced with sheer, unlogical happenstance—or when I don't have all the pieces to play with. My mind still insists on sorting the variables, building an equation, reaching a quotient.

My involuntarily active mind needed distraction. I stretched out on the living room couch and grabbed a book called *Detectionary* from the coffee table, turned to a random page and read about Simon Templar, The Saint. After some time I must have slipped off to sleep, to fuzzy subliminal thoughts about how far removed I was from that fictional detective, or a more recent incarnation, Travis McGee. Leslie Charteris's Robin Hood of Modern Crime, true to his saintly nickname, would look into the story behind Adrian Mallory's nude poses simply because it was the right thing to do, and it might be fun, and he might even end up with pockets lined with the ungodly's filthy lucre. John D. MacDonald's knight in slightly tarnished armor, as the dust jackets have it, would find some way to be prodded into the matter by his omnipresent, over-powering sense of guilt and responsibility.

And then there is Nebraska. No descriptive apellation for this one, please. He isn't propelled by good, or guilt; just greed. The long green. The hope that someone else's misery is deep enough that he—or she—will pay for some glimmer of hope, some fila-ment of help out of it. Cloak it in humanitarianism, slap a coat of "Auld Lang Syne" over it like cheap paint, it still comes down to the same bottom line: lucre. "The struggle for the legal tender." I heard that in a song once. . . .

I woke, hot and sticky and generally uncomfortable, to a room flooded with light. Ten past ten, according to my trusty Timex, which made it just about ten o'clock, but still too late to be able to get away with calling it an early start. Groaning, I snapped off a table lamp and tried to shake from my head the heavy, dull, cling-ing sensation that too little sleep leaves.

I shuffled into the kitchen like an old man and set the kettle boiling, then went and stood under a hot shower that melted most of the kinks from my neck and shoulders but left the fog that socked in the thought centers of my brain and kept anything from taking off or landing there. A few cups of strong black coffee would handle that. Toweling myself, I went back into the kitchen and took the kettle off the flame.

The tap water in that place ran very hot, so I used it to preheat the glass beaker in its metal handle assembly. I measured eight spoonsful of generic coffee into the bottom of the beaker and added water that had just come down from a boil. This I stirred with a knife before I fitted the plunger gizmo into the top of the beaker and let the concoction sit while I went back to the bathroom.

It was too humid to shave with an electric razor; reluctantly I dug out the throat-cutter, put a fresh double-edged blade in it so I could get nicked twice as fast, and lathered up.

I thought about Adrian Mallory, or rather the photos of her. There seemed only two likely possibilities: someone was blackmailing her (or going to) or someone was blackmailing her old man (or going to). I didn't have any trouble with that. I did have trouble figuring how someone like Morris Copel, who would've had to take a rocket to get as high as the bush leagues, connected to something that could result in a great deal of dirty money. Of course, the fact that Copel was dead might've said something about the connection.

Useless speculation: I washed it down the drain with specks of whiskers and shavings of the skin of my throat, combed my damp hair—no point trying to dry it in that humidity—dressed and set out in search of coffee and the telephone book.

Back in the kitchen I lowered the plunger on the coffee pot, pushing the suspended grounds to the bottom of the beaker, where wire gauze on the plunger held them in place, and poured a cup. The advantage of this coffee-making system is the same as its disadvantage: because the coffee doesn't sit and cook, it doesn't turn bitter; but because there's no heat under it, the coffee must be drunk immediately. Or cold. The price we pay.

I took the cup and the pot into the living room, where I sat down with Northwestern Bell's premier publication.

There were plenty of Mallorys listed, but only two with the right initials, and the second of them was an Andrew S. I punched up the first and was eventually answered by a woman who sounded only a little better than I felt. I assumed my most trustworthy tones and asked for Adrian Mallory.

"This is her."

With effort, I restrained the impulse to correct her grammar. Never put the client off with your second sentence. More important, never open yourself to having your own grammatical slips pointed out. I identified myself and quickly added, "I don't think

you know me''—there was, after all, no reason she should remember me from times gone by—"but I think we have a mutual
friend we should get together and talk about.''

There might have been a slight hesitation, or it could have been
my own sluggishness, but it seemed a while before she asked,
"What kind of a friend?"

"I wonder that myself. A friend with a camera.''

Definitely a pause. The kind mystery writers like to describe as
"pregnant."

Her voice, when it reappeared, had gone as flat as last week's
Seven-Up. "Looks like you're in the driver's seat, then,'' she said
dully. "Come on over.''

The line went dead in my ear before I could speak. I cradled the
receiver and poured another cup of coffee, feeling very proud of
myself. Put the heat on 'em, boy. Sweat 'em. Whatever you do,
don't tell 'em you're just trying to sell something they probably
don't need. Shake 'em up and then hit them with the pitch. Why
did I want out of this wonderful business?

In any event, I decided that as long as I was in it I might as well
do it right, and that part of the sweating technique involves giving
the subject time to perspire. So I repaired to my modest but inel-
egant kitchen and threw together a peanut butter omelette, which I
ate with three pieces of English muffin toast and a glass of milk
while figuring my plan of attack. Eventually I rinsed and stacked
the dishes, brushed my bicuspids, poured yet another cup of fast-
cooling joe for the road and headed out.

The day was bright but not sunny; the world was a glare that
assaulted the eyes. I inspected the sky: no danger of rain. Eleven
A.M. and ninety-two degrees already, with humidity to match.

The address in the phone book corresponded to a set of ten-story
sand-colored buildings that jutted up from the side of a gentle
slope set back from the Seventy-second Street strip. I drove around
two or three acres of parking lot before coming upon a building
with the right wrought-iron numbers on it, by which time I knew
why they call such places apartment *complexes:* finding your way
around them is anything but simple.

I stepped into a closet of a foyer, pressed the white plastic stud on the wall next to MALLORY and was buzzed right through the security door.

The place was nice, upscale but not overwhelmingly luxurious. I found the elevator, it found the seventh floor, and I found her apartment. The door opened almost as soon as I rang.

She wore a kind of velour monk's robe, hood down, that sheathed her in pale blue from collarbone to bare feet. Her hair, the color of wheat, was brushed straight back, so severely that I wondered how she could close her eyes. The eyes, which matched her robe, were set in puffy little sacks, probably caused by too little sleep and two or three drinks—one of which was eating a ring into an end table within sight of the doorway. Adrian could have done with a few hours' sleep and some sun, but there was still an underlying natural attractiveness that, as in the photographs resting in my coat pocket, couldn't be ignored.

"You're Nebraska." It wasn't a question; it was a statement wearily made in a low voice that I could imagine being soft and caressing but which was now only bored, flat-sounding, as it had been on the phone.

I agreed.

She stood aside and waved me into the apartment.

Her rooms fitted in with as much of the rest of the building as I had seen—very nice, bordering on the posh. Tall picture windows looked southward toward the angry intersection of Omaha's major north-south thoroughfare, Seventy-second Street, and its east-west counterpart, Dodge Street. Heat made the scene waver outside the glass and I realized with a shiver that the room was almost uncomfortably cold.

Adrian locked the door—chain, dead bolt, doorknob lock-button—and followed me into the room. We stood on a carpet that I recognized from the pictures while she scrutinized me as if I were a newspaper ad. The room was silent but for muffled background noises from the rest of the building, the humming of the refrigerator in the kitchen, the rhythmic ticking of a pendulum clock in the living room.

"So what's the set up?" she demanded after a while. Her esses were a trifle mushy, which they hadn't been on the phone. She'd done a fair amount of drinking in the interim. When I sweat 'em, boy, they sweat.

"The set up?"

"Christ, mister, get with the program! Am I on loan or did he sign over the pink slip?" Her unpainted mouth turned downward at the edges and stayed downturned.

"I must've missed yesterday's exciting episode. Who 'he?'"

Adrian made a disgusted sound and, from the end table, took a glass of liquid so close to the color of Scotch that it had to be Scotch. She took a respectable slug and set down the glass, realigning it with exaggerated, intoxicated care with the moisture ring it had left. "Our 'mutual friend,'" she said scathingly. "Remember?"

"Yeah, him. Well, I should explain—"

"Explain what? That you won me in a card game? Who cares?" Another slug of her drink, then another close look-over. "No camera, huh, lover? Guess the game's changed a little now. Well, never mind. I learn quick, you'll see."

I started to say something clever about the sense our conversation wasn't making, but Adrian shut me up. She shut me up by lifting a delicate hand and drawing her robe's blue plastic zipper, in a single smooth stroke, from throat to navel. The robe slithered to the floor.

Whoever said the camera doesn't lie was right.

She wasn't showing me anything I hadn't already seen, of course, but the suddenness of it, the utterness of it, kicked me hard in the stomach and left me feeling a little breathless and inexplicably foolish.

Adrian's pale nipples rose—but from the cold, not passion. Her voice was totally empty of passion when she spoke. "Well, what's it going to be, lover? You're not going to take any pictures so I suppose he told you you could take . . . me." She spit the final word at me, if it's possible to spit words emotionlessly. Then she stepped clear of the fallen robe and seemed to unfold herself, in a graceful, dancer's movement, until she was supine on the soft carpet, a swatch of sunlight burning gold on her white thighs.

"Come on, honey, what're you waiting for?" Something in her

words—or in the way they were spoken—made me unaccountably ashamed and angry in equal proportions.

"Adrian—"

"Or do you just like to watch? Is that your kick? Then you should've brought a camera, 'cause this is what I'm *best* at." She began to touch herself, her small, high breasts, as if her hands belonged to another, an intimate lover. The caresses strayed downward, lower.

But it was a sham, and suddenly it came apart and the sun danced from her body as she rolled onto her side and curled into a ball and cried.

I gathered her robe, knelt near her head, stroked her yellow hair, witlessly mouthing encouraging things to her. I got her to her feet, got her into the robe, got the robe zipped. She was through sobbing; now she was apologetic: she didn't know what was wrong, she'd be all right in a minute, she needed to have a drink. I told her to shut up, took her to a couch that dozed like a great cat in the sun under the tall windows, sat her down and went looking for something other than liquor to pour into her.

I came back from the kitchen with a cup of tea from a kettle I'd found on the stove. I sat opposite her, on a heavy block of wood that was probably a coffee table, since home altars were out that season. "Drink that," I said, "then we'll talk."

"Talk." Sneeringly.

"It's been known to happen."

"You're being awfully nice to me," she snuffled suspiciously. "How come?"

"I'm working on a merit badge. Drink your tea."

She sipped some dutifully. "I still don't get your game."

"I gathered that." I took the battered brown envelope from my coat pocket and passed it over to her. Adrian took it and peeked inside, but didn't remove the contents.

"Aren't you interested in what's in there?"

"I know what's in there. So?"

"So? So I think you're a lady who's in some trouble, maybe more trouble than she knows what to do with. So I think you could use a little help, which is why I'm here."

Adrian leaned her head against the back of the couch and studied me through red, slitted eyes. "A little help," she echoed. "That's an original approach."

"I thought you'd like it." My fuse was inching short, playing these cat-and-mouse games. I dug out of my wallet the famous laminated photostat that always appears along about page twenty in the private-eye stories. "Look," I snapped, "I'm a private investigator. The mutual friend I mentioned is the man I got the pictures from, a man named Morris Copel. I assume you know him?"

"I don't think so."

Nothing like an honest reproach to slow down a great, righteously indignant speech. "Big guy? Sort of clumsy? Face like someone from Mr. Potato-Head's world?"

She kept gently shaking her head negatively, which thoroughly cooled my jets. Either she was a great little kidder, or she really didn't know Copel—opening the door to some complicated questions I didn't feel like asking myself yet. I doggedly pursued the original course, reading her the *Cliff Notes* on last night's escapades. "Morris Copel, a sort of second-rate citizen, came busting into my place last night. He had been beaten up, shot, and was dying. But first he gave me that envelope. He tried to tell me something about it but in true detective-story fashion he died with the words on his lips. However, I recognized you in the photographs and I figured they meant either you were in some kind of trouble or soon would be. Like I said, that's why I'm here."

Adrian glanced down at the envelope. Looked up at me. Nibbled her lower lip. Sipped some tea. "I see," she finally said. "Well—I certainly do appreciate it."

"Appreciate it?"

"Your bringing me the, you know, the pictures. I really appreciate that."

"And that's it?"

"Well, no. I mean, I'm sorry for the way I acted and everything. I just—well, *jeez,* I just didn't have any idea who you were or what you were or what you came for, you know?"

"I don't know. Who, or what, did you think I was?"

She flushed pink to the roots of her pale hair.

"Exactly. That was a heck of a little show you put on for me, Adrian, and I didn't even ask for it. Think what I could've gotten for the asking. You were willing to do any damn thing I told you to. Why? Because you thought that someone had told me I could tell you to do anything. Morris Copel, I thought, but now I don't think so. You want to tell me?"

She shook her head, violently now, which was all she managed before the waterworks opened again and she ran from the room.

I ran a hand through my hair, feeling dirty, foul. Me, not the hair. The great humanitarian. Here to help. For my next act I'll help little old ladies through intersections they don't want to cross. I stood up and went around the couch to the windows.

Cars slithered like ponderous prehistoric animals on Seventy-second Street. A lot of them rested in the hot glare on the Crossroads shopping mall parking lot. I reminded myself I needed coffee and wondered if I should visit the gourmet department in Brandeis there for something other than whatever was on sale at the supermarket. Meanwhile, the part of my brain that eschewed dealing with such mundanities was wondering furiously about Morris Copel and Adrian Mallory and a set of dirty pictures Adrian seemed only barely willing to acknowledge, even while they were occupying the cushion next to her. Where had Copel gotten the pictures? Who, if not Copel, had taken them? How did whoever persuade Adrian to pose for them? What power over her did he have that made her willing to prostitute herself to me because she thought—merely *thought*—he had given his okay? Why was Copel killed, and by whom? To what use were the pictures being put? And most important, how could I get Adrian to let me— rather, to pay me to—help her?

The answer to that question came first. Adrian reappeared, looking much better except for her eyes, which were surrounded by pillows that you could have had a pretty good fight with. She had loosened her hair and it now hung shimmeringly to her shoulders. Most of the liquor was cried away; a touch of makeup hid what was left, and the sleeplessness.

I opened my mouth but she spoke first.

"I really do appreciate what you've done, and your concern, but I'd like you to go now." She held out a twenty. I must've stared at it. "Don't be offended, please," she said seriously. "You're a professional, you're entitled to be paid for your efforts."

"It wasn't much of an effort. I'd like to do more."

"There's nothing more you can do."

"No, not if you won't let me."

"Listen, I don't need any help, really. Okay, if it'll make you happy I'll admit that things were kind of . . . out of control for a while. Okay? But not anymore. Everything's been really cool for the last couple of weeks, and that's just how I want it to stay. I don't want to stir up anything. I don't want *you* to stir up anything."

It wasn't making any sense. I shook my head and looked back toward the Dodge Street intersection. "It may be out of your hands. A man is dead—"

"Christ, I don't even know who the guy is."

I swiveled back toward her. "He had your pictures."

"So did you, and I didn't know you."

She had a point there.

Time for Plan B. "Look, what about your father? Those photos would be pretty deadly to him if—"

"All right, goddammit," she yelled, "that's *it!* You get the hell out of here, mister, and I mean right now." Wrong tack. She went pink again, this time from raw anger.

I shrugged and headed for the door. "I guess I can't force you to let me help you."

"You got *that* right, at least." She beat me to the door and held it for me. I paused there. It seemed to me I should say something; it also seemed there was nothing to say. Adrian must've felt the same. Her stone look softened a tad and she said, "Hey, don't you think I know it'd kill my father if these pictures got out? And I don't even mean politically. He had a lot of trouble with me when I was a kid, trouble that he didn't deserve. Okay. So now I'm trying. And he's helping me. Despite everything, he never turned his back on me, he never stopped caring, he never stopped loving me. Jeez, this is getting sappy. But it's the truth. Okay? That means it's more important to me than ever to do right by him. I don't know what I'd do if he ever found out about these pictures. Kill myself, maybe. I hope I don't ever have to find out. Well, right now everything's under control, and I don't want it getting screwed up, okay? I'm sure you're a decent guy—you just want to help, right?''

I said, "Yes, but I'm no altruist. I'm in it for the money."

She waved the twenty. "Uh-huh. That's why you jumped at this." She tucked it away in a pocket of her robe. "There's nothing wrong with being a nice guy, Nebraska. God knows, the world can use more of them." She almost smiled. "*I* know it too. But, look, if you really want to help, help by staying the hell out of it, okay? Just leave it alone."

I spread my hands in acquiescence. Nothing I could say would convince her to let me in, let me do what I could to help her through whatever locked her in bondage more cruel than any chains, let me help her take back her own life. In the end I could only comply with her wish: I left her alone. Very much so.

Case closed.

My eyeballs glazed over **3** when I left the refrigerated foyer of the building. Dew appeared on my face. I pushed limp hair back from my forehead and rubbed my eyes. Big improvement. Squinting against the grayish glare, I made toward the old red Chevy. I folded my sportcoat and tossed it into the back seat, then slid in behind the wheel, wincing as hot vinyl stung my back and legs. Without much relish I pointed the wheezing machine toward the Crossroads.

If I subscribed to the same code as the fictional detectives, I'd now be merrily setting off to investigate Adrian Mallory's case, such as it was, on my own, for its own sake. There was plenty to investigate: pornographic pictures of a senator's daughter; the murder of a small-time operator; the daughter's reluctance—hell, refusal—to allow anyone to even try to help; the unknown taker of those photographs; and, less specifically, just what in blazes was going on? All the necessary ingredients of a top-notch little murder mystery. Even your basic handsome, witty detective. In fact, only one element was lacking: the catalyst, that long green stuff with the short life.

Consequently, I was only headed home—too frustrated by the morning's work to wrestle with the crowds at the shopping mall, which I happily sailed past, my mind half-occupied by the tangled swell of traffic, half by Adrian and the matter she wouldn't have me investigate. Arguments I should have made to her flitted belatedly across my steamed-over brain. But I wasn't fooling myself. None would have worked.

Eventually traffic claimed the whole of my attention.

I got tired of a stringy haired, bare-chested high-school parolee and his stringy haired, nearly bare-chested girlfriend insisting that the rest of the world be treated to an unrequested stereo-cassette blast of the B-12s or B52s or whatever that summer's sensation was. I cut them off at the pass, left Dodge Street at the base of the hill where the University of Nebraska at Omaha sprawls, and took the wide, rambling lope along Happy Hollow Boulevard (believe it or not). Its decorative border of big green lawns, big brick houses and big leafy trees gave the illusion of coolness, breeziness. The boulevard deposited me, in time, on the Radial, across from my apartment house. Quite a comedown.

I collected the mail. One of my story payments had finally arrived, along with a group-life offer from a football player, a letter from a computer that was "frankly puzzled" because I had passed up the chance of a lifetime by not entering its sweepstakes the week before, and a picture postcard of the Athens Hilton. It was from Jennifer. I read it on my way up the steel stairs.

She was in Greece, of course, and having a wonderful time.

Again, of course. My wife firmly believed that she was planted on
this green earth for no other purpose than to have wonderful times,
and she applied herself to this end with truly admirable dedication.
Wonderful times, at least by her standards, were scarce in Omaha,
however, and I was surely no fun. Jen had left almost six years
ago—only a few weeks before Copel and the office furnishings
mysteriously vanished. It was quite a couple of months.

Occasionally she came back, presumably to see if I'd come to
my senses yet, if the next time she left for some cosmopolitan
capital it'd be with me instead of yet another of her interchange-
able, well-tanned young men. We had nothing against one another,
you understand—part of the reason, I supposed, neither of us had
pursued the option of divorce—we just each had problems that we
had come to work on, ultimately, apart.

Ironically, our problems were similar: we were each running
from something—or toward something. Who can tell the dif-
ference? I ran by changing jobs and careers; Jen ran by changing
addresses and men. After a lot of years I had come to realize that
what I was fleeing was within me, and with that realization the
need to run evaporated. Jen, apparently, had not yet reached such
a conclusion in her case. I read in her card that she was seeing
Macedonia with someone called Stephan. It was a new name to
me.

Ah, Jen, who could blame you? Not I. The card went on the
bulletin board, along with all the others.

The apartment was as hospitable as the Spanish Inquisition. I
flung open all the windows—even the patio doors, to the immediate and obvious delight of every winged insect within one hundred
miles, who swarmed through the wrecked screens. An ancient
electric fan was pressed into whining service.

I opened a bottle of beer. Thought about Jenny. Didn't like that.
Thought about Adrian. Didn't like that. Thought about The Book.
The check that had just come, and the one that was allegedly on its
way, meant that I could eke by, though hardly in lavish comfort, a
little longer. I certainly could have used the fee I'd hoped for from
Adrian, but if I skimped on luxuries like groceries I could pay the

rent and still have a week, maybe two, to devote exclusively to The Book before I had to get cracking on a magazine assignment due the end of August. Large blocks of time like that are about as common as charitable collection agencies. When you freelance for a living, you come to accept what sacrifices you have to make in order to grab at them.

Eagerly, I found my rough notes on the novel, looked them over quickly—I need at least a general idea of where things are headed, even if they ultimately wind up somewhere else—then rummaged for a pen and yellow pad with which to begin blocking out the next sequences.

Two hours later I looked up. It was 2:30 and the sun had crawled over to the other side of the building, leaving the room considerably dimmer. But no cooler. I remembered reading somewhere that the Chinese advise drinking something hot in order to cool off, so I made a fresh half pot of coffee. The Chinese have the right idea, of course: hot drink makes you perspire, evaporation of perspiration cools. What I forgot was that the air was already supersaturated with moisture, and sweat had no place to evaporate *to*.

I dumped the coffee and took another Falstaff from the fridge. The heck with the Chinese.

Just about then footfalls clanged up the stairs outside. They *tap-tap-tapped* toward my door and were followed in due course by a sharp rap on the aluminum frame.

Behind the rap was a young woman, perhaps twenty-eight, with long, curly dark hair and an attractive face—as near as I could tell, because half her face was hidden by goggly opaque sunglasses that made her look like some kind of insect woman from Mars. She was dressed casually in sandals, denim skirt and a T-shirt decorated with the Electric Light Orchestra spaceship in faded reds and blues and yellows. She was small and trim, and held herself in a fashion that suggested total self-assurance.

I ambled over.

"Mr. Nebraska?" she asked in a voice that had a grain to it, like fine wood. "My name is Marcie Bell."

It sounded like something out of Disney, but I didn't comment; *I* should make fun of people's names? She wasn't dressed for door-to-door sales so I owned up to my identity and asked what I could do for her.

"I need to talk to you about what happened here last night."

"Oh?" Innocently.

"May I please come in?"

I let her in. She took off the goggle glasses and I saw I was right: she was attractive. Not pretty, however. You had to take in the whole picture. If you studied her too closely, you realized that her nose was a little too big, her mouth a little too masculine, her face a little too broad—and so on. Taken together, it worked. Though Marcie Bell would never be described as "beautiful" in the classic sense, she seemed to charge the very atmosphere with sexiness. I offered her a beer, which she accepted, and we eventually settled in the tiny cluttered living room that I hilariously refer to as my office.

"Now," I said, "what about 'what happened here last night?'"

It didn't seem to be the opener she expected. "Didn't— Well, I read it in the morning paper."

I'd forgotten the nightside *World-Herald* reporter. "I take the evening paper," I said. "I tend to forget there is a morning paper."

"There practically isn't," she said, which sparked a laugh that put us over the awkwardness.

"Okay, so what can I do for you?"

"The paper called you a writer, but the city directory has you listed as a private detective," she answered a trifle obliquely.

"You're very thorough," I said casually, while mentally, hopping up onto my toes. "I'm sort of in the process of retiring from keyhole-peeping. However, I can recommend some fine investigators, if you like."

Her dark eyebrows drew down over her dark eyes. "I already have a private detective. Had, I mean. I thought maybe you were working with him. His name was Morris Copel."

I straightened myself in the armchair I occupied. "I wasn't, and that he was working for you is news to me. Have you contacted the police?"

Marcie Bell shook her head.

"Why on earth not?"

She sipped her beer before answering and it occurred to me, apropos of nothing, that it was cloddish of me not to have given her a glass. "I hired Copel the day before yesterday," she said, "and he was supposed to call me today with a report. But I read in the paper that he was killed last night. You were quoted in the story, so I looked you up and found out you're a detective, too. I thought maybe Copel had called you in as a consultant or whatever, and I was hoping you'd know if he had something to tell me. So I decided to talk to you before I talked to the police." She made it sound on a par with deciding whether to have apple or cherry pie for dessert.

"The police are going to be offended that you waited," I said, amazed at her casual manner. Amazed and, I admit, a little impressed. You'd've thought she went through this sort of thing every other Tuesday. I thought she'd made a stupid decision, but I liked the go-to-hell attitude it seemed to imply.

She might've sensed that. A little smile attached itself to her too-wide mouth. It was girlish or wicked, depending how you looked at it. "Well," she said slowly, slyly, "maybe I take the evening paper, like you, so I won't even find out about it for another three or four hours." The little smile grew up and she showed me a lot of ivory teeth. I smiled right back, but behind mine all the familiar warning lights were going on, part of the alarm system you develop after years of dealing with "types." Calculating-type, the lights flashed about Marcie Bell. Don't put your hands through the bars.

"I'm afraid Copel died before he could tell me anything," I said. I didn't mention the negatives; why should I? "Could I ask what he was investigating for you?"

She toyed with a gold serpentine chain around her neck. A tiny gold crucifix dangled from it. "You can *ask*," she said ambiguously. "But why? Are you interested in taking over the case?"

"Not necessarily," I hedged. What I was interested in, of course, was whether or how Adrian Mallory's pictures added into the new equation that seemed to be forming before me. "I'm just curious," I said. "It's none of my business, of course, except," I added significantly, "that Copel did seek me out before he cashed it in."

You could almost see her take the hook, and deep. With someone of a different "type" I might've felt bad about setting her up so blatantly. But turnabout's fair play, they say. So out went my little piece of psychological bait, and Marcie snatched it before it even broke the surface. "You think he was coming to talk to you about my case?" she said, losing the fight to keep eagerness out of her eyes and voice.

"He wasn't coming to look at my scrap books."

She hesitated, but self-interest or selfishness had already goaded her into deciding to confide in me, even against her better judgement. "My brother's disappeared. I hired Copel to look for him." The words tumbled out of her like circus midgets spilling out of a Volkswagen.

"Then tell me about it." Unnecessary prodding; she could no more stop the wordflow than you can decide to stop your next heartbeat.

Marcie Bell nodded. "Why not? I've been through it already with Copel; it's still fresh in my mind." She adjusted her denimed backside into a more comfortable story-telling position. "You kind of have to know Eddie," she began. "He was never much of one to stay put. He no sooner hit the legal age than, bang! he was out of school and on the road. I don't think he's spent more than a year in any one spot since then. Had the wanderlust from the beginning, Daddy used to say." I cringed. Come the revolution, anyone over the age of ten who uses the words *daddy* and *mommy* to refer to his parents will be incarcerated; anyone who uses *mummy* in reference to anything not in the Egyptology section of a museum will be shot.

In any event, Eddie Bell, it seemed, was a drifter who could be expected to drop into your life with all the predictability of a light-

ning bolt—and stick around about as long each time. Almost six
months ago his trail had taken him through Omaha again. "Usually he just takes over my couch," Marcie told me, "but this time
he found a place of his own after a week or so—just a little fleabag
apartment house downtown. He seemed to be planning to stay a
while. But a couple weeks ago he just up and vanished."

"From what you tell me, that's not unusual for him."

"Not if he's going to be gone a few days, or even a week. Any
longer than that, though, he'll always let me know. Eddie may
roam, and we're not really what you'd call all that close, but he's
never really out of touch with me. These last four years, we're the
only family each other has."

"Did you go to the police?" I asked her again.

She looked past me and out the front door. "Not . . . exactly."

"It's a yes-or-no question," I said irritably. "You can't 'not
exactly' go to the police. I'll assume you didn't. How come?"

She looked away from the door and back at me. "I can trust
you, can't I?"

"Probably." Ask an idiotic question . . .

She took a breath. "Eddie's no angel, as you may have
guessed," she said. "Fact is, he's been in trouble with the police a
few times. Never anything really serious—drunk driving, pot
smoking, selling a little. That sort of thing. So—just in case—I
didn't want to go to the police."

"And that's why you hired someone like Copel."

"You mean a private detective?"

Very smooth. I shook my head and smiled in appreciation.
"Guess again, Marcie. Let's quit dancing around it, hmm? You're
a sharp woman—the city directory and all that—so you know that,
legally, Copel was as much a private detective as I am a Miss
America finalist. Why would you hire someone like that instead of
a genuine P.I.? Because you know that a legit eye, even a slightly
shady one, who had any interest in keeping his license and keeping
out of the slammer—which is to say all of them—would call the
cops right now if he went looking for your brother and found him
in the middle of something illegal. I know that all the good TV

shows are packed with contrary indications, but trust me: most
private cops are fond of the habit of eating, and they find it diffi-
cult to support if their licenses are yanked.

"But someone like Morris Copel—who not only had no license
to lose in the first place but who was only infrequently on this side
of the law—has no such moral compunction. As I'm sure you
realized." Marcie was frowning again, but thoughtfully, not angrily. "You stop me when I've told a fib," I added.

She seemed to become aware of her frowning and quit it.
"Don't worry," she said. "I will."

"Good. So what have we got? Your brother, Eddie, disappears
and you send Copel after him and Copel comes back with altera-
tions. If I were to venture an uneducated guess, I'd say Eddie is
for certain involved in something . . . unpleasant, at least."

Her rather boyish mouth set itself and she shook her dark head.
"No," she insisted with quiet firmness. "I told you, Eddie's never
been involved in anything serious—certainly nothing that anyone
would get killed over. My God, we're talking booze and dope—
grass! That's kid stuff."

I didn't tell her that kid stuff like that can have long and sticky
lines that end in unsavory places where people could and often did
get hurt. Instead, I said, "What do you think he's involved in
now?"

"I don't know that he's involved in anything," she repeated.
You had to admire her loyalty. "But I don't want to involve the
police anyhow. Like I said, just in case."

"Very sisterly of you," I said. "Unfortunately, Copel's killing
complicates it a mite. See, the police are kind of wondering why
the man was worked over and finished off. What he was working
on when he got it—that is, your brother's disappearance—probably has a better-than-even chance of shedding some light on it.
There's a Lieutenant Oberon in the Walnut Hill station house,
practically around the corner, who I can guarantee will give you
and your story his undivided attention."

She made a clicking sound with her tongue against the roof of
her mouth. "Maybe I'd better talk to Lieutenant Oberon."

"Maybe you'd better, because he's a good man and he'll probably unravel this thing back to you anyway, at which time his feelings'll be hurt because you wouldn't come see him voluntarily. I'm being a wise-ass, but it's true. Make it easy on yourself and go see Oberon before he comes after you."

"I'll do that," she said with certainty. "But what about you? Are you going to look for my brother?"

"The cops'll do that. For free."

"The cops have a lot to do, including solving at least one murder. And Daddy used to say, you get what you pay for."

"Daddy seems to have had something to say for every possible occasion. Was he with Hallmark?"

She ignored it. "What do *you* have to say about *this* occasion?"

I'd been stalling, mostly because, while I didn't give two hoots for her brother's disappearance or even Copel's death, the two events were obviously linked, and the case looked to be entwined with Adrian Mallory's—which I *was* interested in, though I can't tell you why I should've been. Besides, though I'd hoped to spend some time on The Book, I was still a little short in the bucks department, and Marcie Bell could help out there.

"All right," I said. "I'll need a photograph of Eddie, an address and a retainer." What the hell, I thought. The kid was probably shacked up with some cookie someplace. I'd track him down in a day, two at the outside, and plunge back into my major opus with a freer mind.

"I could only find one picture of Eddie," Marcie was saying as she rummaged through a purse bigger than some Sears stores, "and I gave it to Copel. I'm sure I have others, they're just packed away somewhere. Should I look?"

"It'd be a help," I said, unhappy with the idea of looking for someone I didn't even have a snapshot of. "Can you at least describe him to me?"

"He looks a lot like me, only he's taller and skinnier. Same coloring, though, and people say we look the same around the eyes and mouth." She passed me a slip of pink notepaper on which she'd written Bell's address in blue block letters.

"Do you have a key to the place?"

"I had one, but I gave that to Copel, too."

I didn't much like that, either. It turned a simple look-see into breaking and entering, and Oberon would be unhappy enough that I was easing into the fringes of his investigation. If I crossed paths with him, a B&E would be about all he'd need to put me away until I had a long white beard down to the floor. I pushed that out of my head—Oberon had no knowledge of Bell's existence, much less Copel's involvement in the matter. Yet. Besides, I had every intention of steering clear of the lieutenant.

Marcie peeled a leaf from a checkbook covered in yellow plastic that was supposed to resemble wicker weaving. "Is this enough? It's what I gave Copel."

The check was drawn on an Omaha bank. The amount was enough to get started on. I said as much and added, "If it takes that long, I'll need the same every other day, plus expenses."

She sucked some humid air through her teeth and made it sound sexy. "That's a lot more than Copel needed."

"Yeah, and look what all you got from him. Like Daddy said, you about get what you pay for."

"Okay," she finally, dubiously, said. "But that means I better see some results *fast*. When will you get started?"

I folded her check away. "Just as soon as I get off the phone to your bank."

Actually, I was out the door **4** and down the steel stairs as soon as I saw Marcie Bell's green Le Car make the turn from Decatur onto the Radial, heading south. I hopped into the old Chevy and pointed it in the other direction, up the steep Decatur hill to Military Street, threading through neighborhoods that had seen better days many, many days ago. I ended up on Burt Street where it curves past the sand-colored edifices of Creighton University, standing as its own monument to alumni donations.

Eventually I was downtown, on Fifteenth near the Missouri River, literally in the shade of the I–480 overpass. Eddie Bell's address translated into a lonely old three-story brownstone that should've been razed decades ago. Maybe they were waiting for the wind to take care of it: the firetrap looked like the next stiff breeze would do it in. With the weather as it had been, though, there was no immediate worry.

I parked across the street, near a Safeway that had been converted into a salvage operation. A mangy, scarred bulldog yapped at me from the other side of a chain link fence with double spikes at the top. From somewhere inside the ex-supermarket a black woman's voice slashed through the incessant drone of traffic on the ramp overhead. She had plans for the dog if he didn't shut up. The dog ignored her.

I crossed the pockmarked street and mounted the brownstone's crumbling steps. The elements had bleached the old wooden door to a faded roughness. Some optimist trying to convince a breeze to enter the place had propped the door open a foot or so with a chunk of asphalt from the street. I went in.

Marijuana, cooking-grease and urine, in that order, hit me as I came through the door. To say the place was terrible is unfair to terrible places. The joint was dark and dingy, evil-smelling, run down to the point where it was practically a caricature of run-downness. I didn't want to believe that people lived in such places. But the odors, the few names on the chipped and jimmied mailboxes in the first-floor hall, and the faraway, tinny sound of AM radio wouldn't allow me the fiction.

Eddie Bell's room was on the top floor. I went up a couple flights of stairs that looked as if they might've been new when Roosevelt—Teddy—was president, skirting a large black char where the stairs and part of the wall had been marred in a long-ago fire, staying clear of the peeling walls and dusty, littered corners.

The room I wanted was the last one along the hall. From another apartment on the floor came, loudly, the tinny music I had heard downstairs, the Commodores, oozing through the smudged gray walls like they weren't even there.

A long time ago the door to Eddie Bell's apartment had been white; now it was a color there's not even a name for. There was no number, only the ghostly after-image of one that had fallen off long since. I knocked sharply, authoritatively. No noise, except for the Commodores. I knocked again. The Commodores got a little louder. Back down the hall an emaciated blonde of sixteen or seventeen was standing in an opened door, one bikinied hip thrust aggressively, meager breasts prodding defiantly at a soiled T-shirt. Her parody of sexiness was more than a little depressing. Her hair, her hands, and her feet were filthy. I had the quick and suffocating impression that filth coated everything in this place—including me, eventually, if I stayed too long.

I walked half the distance toward her.

"I'm looking for the man who lives here," I said.

Her unpainted mouth parted in a sneer. "I figured." The Commodores quit behind her and were replaced by a black man's bass voice growling and buzzing against the radio's cheap speaker.

"Is he around?"

"He didn't answer his door, did he? Guess maybe you'll have to come back later." She was a tough little piece, she thought, with a chip the size of the Woodman Tower on her shoulder.

"Maybe I'll just talk to you instead," I said importantly, taking a few more steps her direction and reaching for my wallet. "I'm Sergeant Preston of OPD Narcotics—"

I had the wallet out but before I could show her the badge that wasn't there, she sputtered, "Hey, man, I don't know nothin' about that one. I don't even know his *name*. Me and my old man, we mind our own business." The door went shut like it was on a spring and I heard a chain rattle into place behind it.

Before putting my wallet back I took out my Brandeis credit card. Then I went to Bell's door and used the plastic strip in a way that the department store hadn't intended. No feat; in that neighborhood any eight year old can do the same thing. Probably faster.

The room—it was only one room, with a curtained-off semi-alcove for a kitchen—exhaled bottled-up heat as soon as I opened the door. I shut and locked the door behind me and took off my sport coat. No one would have his windows shut tight in heat like we'd been dragging ass through, but Bell's were latched down until I opened them wide. The current heat wave had begun over a week ago. No one had been here since then. *Lived* here, I corrected myself. I had to keep in mind that Copel had likely been here before me. I threw my coat on the unmade sofabed and started poking around.

The kitchen contained a sink of dirty dishes resting like sunken ships in cold gray water; a gas range; a clattering fridge; a mouse that beat it under the stove when I parted the faded flower-print curtains; a loaf of moldy bread the mouse had been lunching on; a bottle of milk that had gone beyond sour in the icebox. Sherlock Holmes would have known how long that took; I had no idea. An empty rye bottle and the bag it came in were in the grocery sack that served as a wastebasket.

In the living room was the bed that you were supposed to fold into a couch by day, a sad-looking green armchair with a crooked antimacassar, a flimsy coffee table and a floor lamp. In the chair a newspaper, folded to the Ak-Sar-Ben racing results, had gone stiff and was yellowed on the side facing the nearest window. It was the July sixth morning edition of the *World-Herald*. Today was the seventeenth.

I continued my circuit. Nothing to the sofabed but coarse sheets. A cheap clock radio on the windowsill near the bed had the correct time. On the wall near the door was a grime-caked rotary telephone, and next to it was one of those laminated cards on which messages can be written in crayon and wiped away. Superimposed on the remnants of old messages, one remained in a greasy scrawl:

CRZ AL

GEO BAR

7TH 10:30

I took out my notepad and copied it line for line, letter for letter.

If the last line referred to the seventh of July, it, plus the newspaper in the chair, plus what Marcie had told me, indicated that Eddie Bell had indeed disappeared—from this apartment, at least—a little less than two weeks ago. I put away my pad and went on with the breaking and entering.

Behind an unpainted door on which was tacked a poster of John Lennon with orange and purple swirls in his glasses instead of lenses, was a narrow, shallow closet. Two pairs of blue jeans hung on wire hangers alongside three short-sleeved sport shirts. Two empty hangers hung there also, waiting. At the back of the closet was a four-drawer cardboard dresser; it held some T-shirts, underwear, one necktie and a rubber-banded bundle of papers—letters from his sister, birth certificate, draft card and the like. On the closet's overhead shelf was a battered brown suitcase. I took it down, put it on the bed and opened it.

It held a large Hush Puppies box and a Minolta 35mm camera, with flash, in a case.

The box contained a few dozens strips of negatives, fifteen or twenty prints, and a folded sheet of lined paper on which someone had laboriously printed the names and addresses of what sounded like sex shops, adult-book stores and theatres.

I had a sudden, if in retrospect obvious, gestalt, and excitedly began holding the color negatives to the light of the dirty windows. They were pictures of the sort Adrian Mallory had posed for. That, then, had to be the game: Eddie Bell was in the dirty-picture business. He apparently had several women besides Adrian posing for him—whether they cooperated as reluctantly as Adrian I couldn't say—and, judging by the list in the box, hawked the finished product to local dealers. The prints were perhaps samples—or favorites that Bell kept for his own use. Photos of Adrian were not to be found, either as prints or negatives.

Which didn't mean none had ever been there. I reminded myself yet again that Copel had had a key to this joint. I couldn't assume he hadn't been here before me—though I'd come across nothing that suggested the place had been disturbed since its tenant left it—

hadn't found the photos of Adrian, hadn't taken them. In fact, given the events of the previous night, it seemed possible that Copel had done just that.

But why? What was he doing with them—or going to do with them before his plans got changed? And who changed those plans for him, and why?

I was learning something about this investigation: no matter how many different ways I found of phrasing the same old questions, no answers jumped out at me.

The photos went back into the box. I picked up the camera and peeled the case away from it. It was loaded. I took some shots of the inside of the lens cap to finish the roll, unloaded the camera, then replaced it in its case. I put the camera back into the suitcase, put the suitcase, now lighter by the weight of the shoebox, back into the closet.

Shutting the closet door, I leaned against it and thought a moment. There was something out of synch here, something, or things, that didn't seem to fit together properly. I couldn't get a handle on it, so, nettling though it was, I let it go and left.

My girlfriend's music was still playing down the hall, but I saw no sign of her as I left the apartment, weaved down the creaking stairs and through the ancient odors, and on out onto the steaming pavement. There was no sign, either, of the bulldog: perhaps the shrill woman made good on her threat. I locked the shoebox in the Chevy's trunk, started the car and went looking for a phone booth. There had been no telephone directory at Bell's. A certain irony there, I thought.

Neither was there one in the first booth I tried. The second booth lacked a phone, but the book was intact. I checked the taverns listed in the Yellow Pages: no George's Bar or any other name that resembled the GEO BAR scribbled on Bell's wall.

I went back to the car and dug out the prints and address sheet. The sheet listed seven establishments, all with names like The Body Shop and Eros and Studio 69. Most were located in a depressed slice of downtown, not far from where I was. I put the car in a public lot—it was after five so the meter was free, which is

one of those little things that just impress the hell out of clients—
and with the prints and the list in my pocket hiked over to the
nearest address, a "XXX-Rated" theatre called Studio 69.

Of course, it wasn't a true theatre. When I was a kid, it was the
best barber shop on Capitol Street. Now its big window was whitewashed over and festooned with sophisticated marketing slogans
like NONSTOP HOT ACTION and ADULT ENTERTAINMENT and SEX-
PLICIT BOOKS 'N' MAGAZINES.

I went in nevertheless.

The place was divided into halves. The first half, the "lobby,"
sold the promised sexplicit books 'n' magazines, as well as 8mm
and Super-8 films and still photographs. The photographs were at-
tractively displayed in two cardboard boxes atop an uncertain-look-
ing card table to which was taped a handwritten sign: *$2.00 EA.*
Beyond the table was a windowless door through which came am-
plified moans and the steady *click-click-click* of a projector. The
"theatre."

A fat old man with jet-black hair on his head and gray hair on
his arms and neck, sitting in a chair tilted almost to the point of no
return, watched the place. He was reading a magazine whose cover
lines were in Swedish. Two other men—one probably underage,
the other about my age—browsed through magazines and books,
respectively. There was no telling how many, if any, the theatre
held.

"Dollar to look, five dollars for the movie," the fat man recited
without looking up from his literature. I gave him a buck, which
he deposited in a strongbox on the cobwebbed radiator next to his
chair. When he reached across I saw the butt of a gun under the
tail of his untucked sport shirt.

"You seen Eddie lately?" I asked casually.

He looked sourly at me. "I don't know you."

"Of course you don't. Eddie always handles this end of the
business."

The fat man went back to his magazine.

I leaned over him. He smelled of bay rum and old sweat.
"Look," I said in a confidential tone. "There's no problem. Ed-

die—Eddie Bell—he's my partner. We make pictures, y'know, like those over there. Like these here.'' I took the prints from my coat and spread them out for him like playing cards.

He didn't say anything, didn't even move, except for the eyes. They swiveled like ball bearings in oil, away from the naked adolescents on tandem bikes and toward the pictures of naked women posing alone and in pairs. His pupils dilated. A man who loves his work, I thought.

"Anyhow," I was saying, "I take care of the . . . creative side"—he looked up and I winked—"and Eddie takes care of the business side. Only Eddie skipped out on me, and he owes me some money. So I'm looking for him. I got his list of contacts and this place is on it. I figure he's probably still selling our stuff—my stuff—and pocketing my share, too. Maybe he's been by."

"Maybe he has," said the old guy. "I'm not the boss here."

"Who is the boss here?"

He went back to the magazine.

I put away the photos and took out my wallet. He eyed it furtively over the top of his reading, then locked his baby blues resolutely onto the page, like a bluenose avoiding the near occasion of sin. Sort of.

Sighing, I pocketed the wallet. "You mind if I look through those boxes to see if there's any of my stuff there?"

"You paid your dollar," he said, wetting a pudgy forefinger to turn a page.

So I waded through a couple million dirty pictures. Black-and-white, color, instant, prints, competent, hopeless, boring, titillating, disgusting. In the grand scheme of things I suppose they averaged out to be pretty tame. Still, I felt vaguely soiled by the time I finished sifting through the second box. I couldn't tell you if Eddie Bell's craftsmanship was represented. I didn't give a damn about that except insofar as Adrian's pictures might've been concerned. In that place, at least, they weren't.

However, I had been hired not to find pictures of Adrian, but the man who took them. I grabbed a half-dozen prints at random and took them over to the jolly old fat man.

"He's been here, all right, the bastard," I said, waving the pictures.

"Two dollars apiece," the fat man said lethargically.

"Sure, why not? I'll take it out of that crook's hide when I find him." I handed over a bill.

"Don't you got it exact?" he complained.

"Just the twenty."

Annoyed, he reached for the strongbox.

"Say, you don't happen to know a guy named Morris Copel, do you? Might've been Copel who brought in the pictures."

The old guy gave me a five and four ones—my browsing fee generously returned on the purchase—that looked like they'd been printed during the first week of the second world war and carried in someone's shoe since then. "I told you," he said gruffly, "I only work here. I don't know nobody and I don't know nothing." Up went the magazine like a drawbridge.

I pocketed my change and left.

It was still early—about six-thirty—and the next place on my list was only a few blocks over. I deposited my purchase in a blue-and-white Keep Omaha Beautiful receptacle and walked up Fifteenth Street.

In the next couple of hours I repeated my stellar performance six more times—once in each place on Bell's list, places like the X-tacy Connection and The Retreat, places with bookstores or theatres or peepshows in the back, massage parlors and God knows what all else upstairs or downstairs. I came away feeling very grimy, very tired, and not very knowledgeable. My reception in each establishment was about the same as it had been in the first, as were my results: zip. A curious thing, however: in none of the shops did I come across any photos of Adrian, though I did spot copies of most of the prints I took from Bell's, as well as some others that I was certain, judging by the style—if that's the word—Bell took. The absence of Adrian Mallory's shocking pink epidermis in any of Omaha's more sordid pleasure palaces only reaffirmed my original belief that the photographer had in mind another purpose—namely, blackmail, either of the woman or, more likely, her father.

Which did me a lot of good. I hadn't turned up anything that Adrian didn't already know when she tossed me out on my ear that afternoon. There existed the slim possibility that, if I returned and told her I knew now pretty specifically what her situation was, she'd break down and let me try to help her figure a way out of it. But was it worth the effort?

Besides, I reminded myself, I had a client, one to whom I had so far nothing to report. In fairness to the one picking up the bills, I decided, I should concentrate on *that* matter and give the other one a rest.

What, then, to do about Eddie Bell, who seemed to have vanished off the face of the earth, or at least out of that burg? My best next step appeared to be one that would have been my first step if circumstances had been different. I decided to drop in on OPD and see what they could tell me about Bell. There were other fish in the sea—or on the force—besides Oberon, and at this stage of the operation no one needed to know of the connection between Bell and Copel. I remembered a sergeant in Missing Persons, Grier, who used to make a habit of staying late. Since I was already downtown, I'd see if I could catch him.

By now the shadows would've been getting long—if only there were any shadows. The peculiar thing about these humid days is that, bright as they are, there isn't really much in the way of sunshine. Plenty of heat, however. That, absorbed all day by the asphalt, came up through the soles of my shoes as I crossed the parking lot under those pinkish gray skies.

Only a couple cars besides mine were left in the lot. I paid no attention until, when I was perhaps twenty-five feet from the Chevy, doors opened on a dark green Fairmont parked two slots down on the opposite side of my car. All the little warning lights and buzzers in my head went off at once. Two very large, solid, imposing types unfolded themselves from the Ford.

I checked the impulse to run. The two would be on me before I reached the Chevy, if I chose to run that way. And if I ran in the opposite direction, I had little doubt that they were prepared to pursue me—about as much doubt as I had that they could catch me. I know a little karate that a guy in the service showed me, enough to put on a show and, usually, scare off someone who's more bluff than backbone. Neither of these two trees seemed to fit that category.

My ultimate course of action—to keep walking as if I hadn't noticed them—might appear very brave. In actuality, it was the only option left.

Lew Archer or Philip Marlowe or some other high-powered sleuth would by now be surreptitiously adjusting their clothing in order to quickly draw their .45s or whatever, and drill the opposition into submission. Me, I don't like guns much. They smell. They're greasy. They make a lot of noise. People who hang around them seem to end up with new orifices in them. Oh, I know my way around them okay—I carried all sorts of big, bad things in Vietnam—and I own a couple handguns. Had one with me now, in fact. Locked safely away in the glove box of the Chevy.

I was armed only with my sunny disposition.

And so I walked.

The car keys were already in my right hand. I furtively manipulated them so that two jutted out between the first and second fingers of my fist, two between the second and third.

One of the imposing men—a big, square black man who looked like he could play for Nebraska—stayed close to their Ford. The other—who but for color might have been the first's brother—rounded the front of my car, not accidentally putting himself between it and me.

I made myself stroll as if he weren't there. I heard the blood in my ears, imagined I felt the adrenaline being dumped into my system, fought to keep my knees solid.

And I walked.

At a distance of about eight feet the white man held up a hand the size of a frying pan. "Are you the owner of this car?"

I stopped and stared him down. It's like they tell you about dogs: don't show your fear. It's all very psychological and stuff, and probably more effective if your legs aren't made of Silly Putty.

"Me and the Omaha National," I said—casually, I think. "Why? You want to buy it?"

He ignored that and said, over his shoulder, to his companion, "It's him. Call the Lieutenant." He rotated his two hundred pounds back toward me as he reached into his coat pocket. He flashed the badge. "Oberon wants you."

My stomach unknotted and turned nauseated on the excess of unused energy it now had to absorb. "Christ," I breathed fervently. "Don't any of you guys wear uniforms anymore?" I took a couple breaths. "What's Oberon's problem? What's so hellfire important he couldn't't've left a message on my machine?"

"I wouldn't know. The word just came over the air that we should keep an eye out for this vehicle"—he gestured vaguely toward the Chevy—"because Oberon wanted to talk to its owner. My partner and me were just coming back from a call when we spotted it here. We figured you'd come back to it pretty soon, since 'most everything closes down here at night." He shrugged halfheartedly. "Sorry if we upset you."

"Next time try a note on the windshield, okay?"

The other one came out of the unmarked car. "I talked to Oberon. He wants to see the gentleman right now."

"We'll run you over there, sir," my cop said preemptively.

"Thanks, but it's just not as thrilling when you don't have the bells and whistles and the little gum machine on top. Besides, it's on my way anyway."

He was unconvinced.

"Look, if I bolt, Oberon'll just send you guys looking for me again, right? Give me a little credit. Besides, there's no charge against me; I'm not under arrest—or am I?"

They talked it over between them with their eyes, the way people who work together a great deal can. "We'll tag after him," the black cop said.

"Wonderful," I said, "a police escort."

5

OPD Walnut Hill head- quarters on Fortieth Street is a graceless block of dark red brick, wired-glass windows and steel doors, all half hidden by towering walnut trees. It was perhaps a ten-minute jaunt from where I was, and my official chaperones dogged me the whole distance. Kids were still out—it was only about nine, even if my body thought it was midnight—and they played on bikes and skateboards in the street, but listlessly, wilted by the heat. I parked a half-block from the station and, under the watchful eyes of my guardian angels, negotiated the buckling side-walk.

Here was none of the noise, commotion, drama and glamour of a big city's—or a television series'—precinct house. Walnut Hill, at least at that time of day, reminded you more of a dilapidated office building, or of a business that was about to go under for the second, maybe third, time. Perhaps a half-dozen people loitered in the halls. The place was almost as exciting as the county morgue at 2 A.M.

The desk sergeant nodded knowingly when I told him my name and my business. He had me sign in, then gave me a visitor's tag and directions to Oberon's office.

Cubicle, more like it. It was one of those partitioned affairs, no doors, pressed-wood walls that start a foot above the floor and come to about nose level and are topped off with eight inches or so of frosted glass. Oberon's cubicle, at the end of a narrow, dusty corridor lined with identical offices, was about as roomy as a good-sized broom closet. Into it was crammed a steel desk, a desk chair, visitor's chair, coat rack, chipped green two-drawer file and two of those brown cardboard boxes you use when you've filled your cabinet. And, of course, Oberon. All the trappings of power.

He looked up from a manila folder as I came through the doorway. A cigarette burned in an ashtray, surrounded by its fallen comrades. I sank silently into the company chair and Oberon took a drag from the cigarette before smearing it out. "So it's you."

"So it is. The lollipop guild made it seem pretty important. Not to mention mysterious."

"There's no mystery to it." Oberon's voice was tired and tight, totally empty of the wry reasonableness that was usually there. Something was wrong and, though I didn't know what it could be, I had a feeling I'd soon be informed.

"No mystery at all," he continued. "I asked you very nicely to keep your nose out of the Copel case. Next thing I know there you are with your nose in the Copel case." Anger—and, I have the conceit to think, hurt—throbbed just beneath the surface of his words, pumping up the volume behind them. His voice echoed from the hard walls. Self-consciously, he reduced the decibels, which only made him sound all the more dangerous. I had known Ben Oberon for ten or twelve years; this was the first time I'd ever thought of him as dangerous. I didn't like it. Primarily because I knew he was completely justified.

He lit another cigarette, his watery eyes locked on me. "Give me one good reason I shouldn't lock you up and lose the key."

In Eddie Bell's apartment I had had the same eerie feeling I was getting now—like I was looking right at something but couldn't see it, an aggravating what's-wrong-with-this-picture sensation. Until things started to sort themselves out, I decided to curb my natural tendency toward smartassery.

"Because I'm not guilty," I said reasonably.

"What's that, then?"

"I'm answering your question. We should be friends again because I'm not guilty. I'm not nosing into your investigation." Well, not *exactly*.

"Goddammit, man, don't fuck with me!" The words erupted like a thunderstorm, and this time there followed no attempt to quiet them. "Vice had a guy poking around a place called Studio

69—you've heard of it, I assume—on a prostitution complaint.'' I recollected the two browsers in that first store and wondered which it was. "He overheard you mention Copel's name, and the name clicked. He called me, gave me your description, and I knew it had to be you, you bastard.'' Suddenly his temper burst again; the folder in his hands flew against the wall like a Frisbee and spilled multicolored report forms onto the scruffy beige linoleum. "You bastard! You damn son of a bitch, I *believed* you when you said you'd keep the hell out of this.''

Ouch.

"Look, Ben, I don't blame you for being pissed. I'm sure that to you this looks like I've gone behind your back. But it's not that at all. In fact, I was on my way over when your dynamic duo buttonholed me.''

"Uh-huh.''

"Yeah, well, I'm not surprised you don't believe it.'' Of course not; it was a lie. "But it's true. The fact is, I took on a client today. A missing-persons thing. And as I started following up some leads it began to look like there might be some connection with your case. That's why I was asking after Copel. As it is, I came up with goose eggs all the way around—but, naturally, if I'd turned up anything that could've even remotely been useful to you, I'd've told you about it right away.''

"Aren't you generous.'' If you could bottle his tone of voice you'd have a dandy little paint remover on your hands.

"What can I do to convince you, Ben?''

He thought about it over his cigarette. "Who'd you say this client was?''

"I didn't and I won't. You'll have to believe me when I say there is one—I don't work without someone to pay the way—but beyond that, well, you know how it is.''

Oberon snorted. "Yeah, like I know how long that'd stand up in court. Okay, how about this supposedly missing person?''

Moment of truth. I was a little reluctant to part with that information, too. But I estimated I'd gotten away with about all there was to get away with. I'd already told Oberon there *might* be a link between his case and mine; it was only logical he'd want a glim-

mer of what that link might be. To deny him that was to spend the
night—at least—in the slammer. I gritted my teeth and gave the
information. "Fellow by the name of Eddie Bell, bee, ee, double-
el, as in Alexander Graham. Appears to be something of a lowlife
who vanished from the scene a couple weeks ago."

Oberon was frowning, but in concentration. He seemed to be
studying a white chalky mark where the corner of the file folder
had hit the dark wall. "Bell . . . Bell. . . ."

"Is it ringing one?"

He launched himself out of his swivel chair. "Hang on a minute."

I was glad of that; it gave me a chance to relax and concentrate
on getting my heartbeat down to a level I could hear over. I did a
quick stress-reducing exercise: went limp in my chair, eyes closed.
Took a deep, full-capacity breath and let it out, saying under my
breath, "One." I repeated it twice, after which, as usual, I felt
astonishingly relaxed. The key is in concentrating on "one": it
blocks out distractions, including other thoughts. Of course, the
word can just as easily be "word" or "om"; concentration is the
key.

Oberon was back directly with another manila file. I didn't inter-
rupt as he came in and sat down, still reading it. Presently he
folded it closed and looked up at me. "You have any idea what
you're getting into here, boy?" Something a lot like concern had
taken up residence in his voice over the last five minutes. It made
me concerned in return. "If it's the same Eddie Bell, dirty picture
pusher"—I nodded—"the word on the street is that he ran afoul of
some local muscle."

"How? I mean, in what way?"

"They're not saying, or at least not in our earshot. The word
simply is that Bell got into trouble with the Mob."

"Big trouble?"

"The kind for which they make sure you never get into trouble
ever again."

"Wow. What do you have on Bell?" I held out my hand for the
folder.

Oberon's baggy face looked sour. "Be serious." He skimmed

through a few sheets. "Nothing much, and nothing serious. We know that he'd drift in and out of town every so often. Supplied the local shops with dirty pictures. Real big-time; I'm surprised he doesn't have a villa in Rome. Didn't, I guess I should say. Well, we busted him for pot a couple of times, a couple of times on open bottle. Held and released in a kiddie-porn investigation. Seemed to be clean on that score, at least." Oberon closed the file and leaned back in his squeaky chair. "Definitely small potatoes. There are a dozen guys just like him here—here and everywhere else. They never make any money at it. We have better things to do with our time than chase around after every clown with a Polaroid who gets his girlfriend to strip and go along with his fast-buck scheme. But you mentioned something to do with a homicide investigation. . . ."

"Yeah. I have reason to believe that Copel was looking for Bell, too, up until the time he was killed. Until Copel was killed, I mean."

Oberon stopped rocking in his chair, stopped dead still, but other than that made no sign he'd even heard me until he said, "What makes you think that?"

"Because my client tells me he or she hired Copel to look for Bell."

"Terrific—Copel had no license."

No point telling him I thought my client preferred it that way. "It's like a driver's license: you can't drive without one—but you *can*."

The lieutenant chewed on it a minute. Then: "You think Copel's murder has anything to do with Bell, or his investigation into Bell's disappearance?"

I shrugged. "I didn't. But now you tell me that Bell might be dead, too—though you can't tell me why. That's an awful coincidence."

Somewhere along the way Oberon had lost his cigarette. He reached for the pack on the desk, shook one out, then apparently thought better of it. He leaned back in his chair again. "Sure as hell is," he said quietly. "Now you see what kind of trouble you're flitting around in."

"It's a little early to say. So far I've infiltrated a half-dozen sex shops, with nothing to show for it."

"Trying to pick up Bell's trail? How'd you know where to start? I don't figure you as the type who has a great deal of familiarity with these places."

"Thank you for that." I told him about the list I had found in Bell's room. Of course, through it all, I scrupulously avoided any mention of Adrian Mallory or the pictures of her Copel had when he died.

Oberon cocked a narrowed, bloodshot eye my way. "Nebraska, tell me I'm not going to have to be concerned about a breaking-and-entering here."

For someone who professes to hate lying as much as I do, I certainly engage in an awful lot of it—and I'm disturbingly good at it, if I say so myself. "Of course not," I said breezily. "My client provided me with a key."

"Wasn't that thoughtful? And isn't it a swell coincidence that your client just happened to *have* a key?"

"No coincidence. My client has a right to the key; in fact, Bell gave it to him or her. To say anything further would be telling, though."

Oberon grunted. "Gee whiz, we wouldn't want that. So I'll just settle for the key."

That's the trouble with lying, beyond the moral considerations: it's too easy to get caught. "The key, Gracie?"

"Come on, man, I'm trying to do my job and I'm trying to give you a break. The key to Bell's place, let's have it."

I screwed up my face in what I hoped looked like serious pensiveness. In fact, that's what it was: I was thinking furiously of a way to keep Oberon from calling my bluff. "I'm not too sure about that, Ben," I said gravely. "Technically, it's not mine to give; it's my client's property."

"Your client'll get it back." He waited patiently while I stewed over the nonexistent key. Then, an unmistakable edge came back into his voice. "It'll save me some work, you know. Now that we know there's a connection between the cases we'll want to go over that Eddie Bell's place. That is," he added with a sour, sarcastic look, making the loose skin over his eyes and under his mouth bunch up, "if you're *quite* through with it now."

I sighed, reached into my pocket, took out my key ring and started working off the key to the storage locker in the basement of my apartment building. "You realize, of course, this is going to put me in a bad way with my client, who's expecting this back."

"I'll write you a note. Besides, I said he'll get it back. He'll get it back. Quit stalling, already."

I handed over the key. "The thing is, Ben, you already have a copy of that." He gave me a look. "In with Copel's effects. My client previously gave Copel a copy of the key to Bell's place; did Copel have a key ring on him when your guys catalogued his stuff?" I knew damn well he did, having gone through his pockets myself first, but it was good theatre. "Well, there you have it— it's probably on that ring, probably sitting in an envelope in the basement of this building even as we speak. So how about doing me a favor? Give me back that key and use the one you already have."

Oberon toyed with the key, tapping it abstractedly on the manila folder that held Bell's file. "It seems to me I've already done you a big favor by not tossing you into the pokey."

"And I appreciate your generosity, Ben, even if I'm not certain you'd've been so gracious if not for the fact that we both know you haven't got anything on me. However, I'm still grateful, and I'm counting on your famous generosity this one more time." I flashed him my Pepsodent smile, the one Erik Estrada wishes I wouldn't use. If you're going to lay it on, lay it on thick.

Oberon barked a short laugh and began to resemble the cop I knew. He flipped the key over to my edge of the desk. "Criminy, *here,* already. Anything to shut you up."

"Thanks," I said and meant it. The key went immediately into my coat pocket. Out of sight, as they say.

"Okay. Probably couldn't've gotten a search warrant anyway." He fiddled with a Ticonderoga pencil, tapping the erasing end nervously into the palm of his left hand. "Look, I . . ." he started, then stalled out. "I mean—ah, hell, I'm no good at apologies.

I've been sitting on you pretty hard, and I guess I'm trying to say I'm sorry. We've known each other a long time and I suppose I should've given you the benefit of the doubt. But things have been really shitty around here lately and when it looked like you played me for a sucker, I guess I just blew my top, you know?''

I shrugged. "I know. And I don't blame you. It would've looked the same to me, to anybody. Forget it. I just hope what little I've given you helps on the Copel case.''

He made a disgusted sound and a face to match. "Yeah. Well, like I said, I probably can't even get a warrant. Latest bullshit from downtown. Seems there are too many unsolved homicides— too many for an election year, at least. Our marching orders are to clean up the long-outstanding investigations first. Mayor'll look better that way when he debates his opponents. Never occurs to them that if they increase budget and manpower we just might be able to solve more cases altogether. Given the present situation, anything we put on the back burner is liable to fall right down the back of the stove.''

"That's crazy.''

"That's electioneering. If your unsolved investigations only go back two, three months, it's easier for the man to debate on TV than if they go back a year or more.'' He must've changed his mind about the cigarette, because now his long fingers snared one and set it afire.

"I thought you gave up that vile habit years ago.''

"So did I. Guess it's like riding a bicycle—once you learn you never forget.''

"Ah. Well—listen, if there's anything I can do, or even if you just need someone to watch you let off steam . . .''

"Thanks. Really. Don't think I don't appreciate it.

"But now listen.'' He was all business again, stabbing the air with the orange end of his cigarette for emphasis. "I still don't want you poking around this case—thing—whatever it is—especially now. If the word from the street is right, your missing person isn't liable to get found. They're saying he was taken out by Al Manzetti. You know Manzetti?''

"By reputation only."

"Try to keep it that way. They call him Crazy Al, but not to his face. He was the toughest torpedo in Chicago, back when they used to have torpedos, back in the old mob. Homicidal maniac if there ever was one. In fact, the man's too screwy even for the Mafia these days. They don't like gaudy headlines. And I think they're scared of him. Our sources say Manzetti went crazier than usual about three years ago, cut up a ward boss's girlfriend and dumped what was left of her in the Chicago River. It cost a lot to hush that up, and it landed in the papers anyway—no names, of course. That would've been the end of just about anyone but Manzetti. He had too many friends in high places—or at least he had the goods on them—and he was too high up himself. So they busted him and sent him down here—made him a second or third banana on a second- or third-string team. What I'm saying is, this is a guy who doesn't need very much provocation to kill, and now on top of everything else he's carrying a grudge the size of Mt. Etna. He may be the one who took out Copel—Bell, too, maybe. Steer clear of him."

"Don't worry. If I get in a jam I'll call Eliot Ness."

Oberon's eyes rolled back in his head. "That's right, make a joke of it. I'm sure this all seems real comic book to you, wiseass, but these guys exist and they mean business. You fuck around with them and you may find yourself up to your eyebrows in *big* trouble. I ought to lock you up for your own good."

"Which is where I came in." I stood. "If that's it, I'll split now—you seem too determined to let the city put me up for the night." I stopped in the doorless doorway. "Hey, thanks for everything, huh?"

"Uh-huh. And look, what I said goes. Even if this case is on hold, you screw around with it and I will lock you up. Like I said, for your own damn good."

"My pal."

Marcie Bell lived in the top **6** half of a twenty-five-year-old duplex in Westgate, a middle-class neighborhood off Eightieth Street and the Interstate that wasn't even in the Omaha city limits when the house was built. Now it's practically downtown.

The house was white with faded blue trim. A couple of old oaks shielded it from the last light of the day. I matched the address on her check to one of the two identical doors at the front of the place and mashed the buzzer. I heard or imagined activity upstairs. Somewhere a door opened and a voice called, "Come on up." I tried the door before me; it was unlocked, opening to a small entry and a long flight of stairs running straight up to another door—at which stood Marcie. "Hi! This is a shock. Well, come on up!"

I went on up. It was hot on the stairs, and I noticed Marcie's dark hair was damp and clung to her face and neck, which were also moist. It was a look I never found appealing in the fashion ads, where it's used a lot. On her it was distractingly attractive. "Don't tell me you have anything to report already?" I opened my mouth to respond but she preempted me. "Wait, wait. At least come in and sit down first." I went past her into the tiny apartment, into a wall of heat and music. "Make yourself uncomfortable," she advised as she closed and locked the door. "I was just making some tea, but it looks like you can use something stronger."

It was a tempting offer but, dragged out as I was, I knew a drink would about put me away. I declined it and took her up on the tea. As soon as she finished with the door she disappeared into a minuscule kitchen to finish her preparations.

The apartment was small, smaller than mine even, but clean and well-decorated. The door at the top of the stairs opened into a cozy living room with a large picture window looking out into the oaks shading the house. The kitchen, such as it was, was to the left, at the beginning of a short hallway off of which, I assumed, was a bathroom. At the end of the hall was a door to, probably, the bedroom. Not too bad.

I planted myself dead center on a flower-print sofa under the picture window, where I could take full advantage of a stiff breeze whipped up by a square electric fan propped in the window. It chilled me, but that felt good. I rubbed my eyes. The lids' insides felt lined with sandpaper.

Marcie emerged with two amber glasses filled to the top with ice and rapidly cooling tea. "Do you use sugar or lemon?"

"Neither, thanks." I half drained the glass, warm though the drink still was.

She lowered the volume on a small stereo set propped on the top shelf of a boards-and-bricks bookcase, then put on a brass reading lamp. She settled herself on a rattan chair near the couch. "Can you tell me anything about Eddie?"

"I can't tell you where he's gone to; I don't even have a clue. I'll give you that straight up."

"But then—"

"What am I doing here, and at this time of night?" I took another slug of tea. The ice cubes were almost gone and the tea was respectably cold, good on the back of my throat. I was waiting for the caffeine to hit. "Marcie, did your brother mention, or give any indication, that he was in some kind of trouble before he vanished?"

"Trouble? What do you mean, trouble? I told you, Eddie's had a couple run-ins with the police, but nothing serious." She fiddled with the gold chain circling her neck. The crucifix dangling from it glinted gently.

"We'll come back to that one. Right now, I'm not talking about trouble with the police. I mean, did Eddie ever say anything about problems he was having with—well, gangsters?"

Her dark eyebrows fairly disappeared into her hairline. "*Gang-*

sters?'' She sputtered a laugh. "In *Omaha?* You've got to be kidding!''

"Actually, no. Look, Marcie, I'm going to be brutally up-front with you, mostly because I'm too tired to think of smooth ways of putting things. The word on the street is that Eddie got himself into one whole lot of trouble with a local gang boss, a particularly bad character they call Crazy Al, though not, I'm told, within his earshot. Ever hear of him?''

"No," she snapped belligerently. "Why should I have?''

She shouldn't have, except that I was certain, after Oberon's little pep-talk, that the cryptic memo on Bell's wall indicated a meeting with Crazy Al—CRZ AL—on the seventh at 10:30 in a place Bell's personal shorthand abbreviated GEO BAR. It was a meeting from which Bell had not yet returned, and seemed unlikely to.

"Because the word on the street is also that Crazy Al had Eddie killed," I said crudely. "Why this should be I don't know. I'm hoping you do.''

Incredulity had hardened into something very much like shock on Marcie's face. I let her sort through her reactions a minute, maybe two. Finally the shock, if that's what it was, melted into a kind of tight-lipped defiance. "I think you must be crazy," she decided at last.

"It's been suggested before, but that's really not the point. The point is that your brother has for some time now been involved in the taking and selling of pornographic pictures—the police know all about it, and I'm sort of surprised you don't—which may be what put him at odds with the Mob. It's an area they've been known to have an interest in, though not around this town before. I believe your brother was also very likely into something more serious than dirty pictures—blackmail, to be specific—and *that* may have easily led to his troubles with the mob. The problem is, all I can do now is speculate. Unless you have anything helpful to tell me.''

Her face was flushed now, her delicate eyebrows drawn into a taut V over hot eyes that flashed spikes at me. If looks could kill, as they say.

"I have something to tell you all right, mister private detective. You have lost your mind, that's what I have to tell you. You waltz in here and start tossing around some bullshit about my brother being in some porno ring with gangsters. My own *brother!* Don't you think *I'd* know about it?"

"Apparently you don't. Look, Marcie, I know this has got to be a shock. But I'm afraid it's all true. Besides what the cops told me, I found pictures in your brother's place, plus a list of shops he sells them to locally."

"And just how in hell did you get into Eddie's apartment?"

I was getting tired of the course of this conversation: too many detours. "Ah, for God's sake, Marcie, get with the program. Just because your last name's the same as Peter Pan's little friend doesn't mean you have to share her naïveté. Your brother hawked pictures of naked ladies and I broke into his apartment. Nobody's a saint. Face facts."

"I think I'll call the police instead."

I drank some tea. "It's immaterial to me. But I'd think twice if I were you. I just left the cops, and I can say with some certainty that they'd love to get their hands on you. They know about the connection between Copel and your brother. They know Copel was investigating Eddie's disappearance the night he ended up dead in my living room. They figure the one might have had something to do with the other. Now so far I've managed to keep your name out of things. You pick up that phone and you're in it up to your eyeteeth. No turning back. Your decision."

She had half risen from the wicker chair. Now she sat again, heavily, furiously. "You bastard," she spat venomously. "What the hell do you want from me?"

"Respect and admiration, but I'll settle for some straight talk. You say you didn't know anything about Eddie's photographic hobby?"

"That's what I say, and I still don't believe it." For emphasis she crossed her arms under her breasts, which made them swell distractingly under the ELO T-shirt.

"Whatever you prefer. Did Copel and your brother have anything to do with each other before you hired Copel to look for Eddie?''

The question seemed to surprise her. ''No. Why?''

''Because—and I have nothing to back this up, it's just groping on my part—I wonder if Copel and your brother were into a little business prior to Eddie's disappearance. A little blackmail business.'' She started another protest rally but I cut her off. ''Look, when Copel showed up at my place the other night, he was carrying some pictures, nude shots of a young woman whose name you'd probably recognize. I gallantly returned them to her and talked to her about them. She wouldn't tell me anything I'd call useful, but I came away with the distinct impression she had been forced to pose. Why anyone would force her seems a little obvious, don't you think? Well, I searched your brother's room and came up with a mittful of pictures of the same style, if not the same woman, and so I began to wonder if this wasn't putting a considerable strain on coincidence. What do you say?''

Her tea had gone untouched. Now she picked it up but did nothing with it, as if she'd forgotten what you do with a glass of tea. She put her head against the back of the chair and looked at the ceiling. ''I don't know what to say. I still can't believe Eddie is mixed up in anything that—that bad. I don't know . . .'' She stood and left the room, excusing herself. I put my own head back and closed my burning eyes. What a day. I was exhausted enough that the idea of giving Marcie Bell her money back and calling it all quits occurred, and appealed, to me. But I knew that wouldn't work—I'd be a candidate for the looney bin inside of forty-eight hours if I didn't take things to a point where they at least *started* to make sense. . . .

And then it was dark, and close. I suffered a moment's disorientation before realizing I had fallen asleep on Marcie's couch. The perfect guest. I tried to catch a stray moonbeam on my wristwatch: 11:30. I hadn't been out *too* awfully long.

I sat up and rubbed my neck, still foggy-headed and uncertain what to do. I had already violated etiquette to the point that I could probably just lay it to rest now and slink silently into the night. On the other hand, I felt I should at least thank my hostess for the loan of the couch.

Being unsure of the lights' location I left them out and negotiated my way to the short hallway without knocking anything over. At the door to the bedroom I paused. No light seeped under the door, no sound came through it. I tapped softly, almost silently. No reply. In I went.

The room was heavenly cool. A window air conditioner hummed happily away on low. Above it, through the top half of the window, street light stumbled in and painted the room indigo. I could discern a tall chest of drawers, a smaller dresser with mirror, a night stand, a bed. On the night stand a clock radio played soft music at a volume so low as to be virtually inaudible over the quiet hum of the cooling unit. On the bed a body under a pale sheet stirred slightly.

"Don't let the heat in," she slurred sleepily in a voice barely louder than the music.

I stepped into the room and shut the door behind me. The room was small; that single movement put me at bedside. "I must've left my manners in my other pants," I said by way of apology. "I usually don't go around conking out in people's living rooms."

"'S okay. I guess it's been a long day for you."

"You too. I'm sorry about—well, about out there."

"I know. Me too. I just . . . I don't know. I'm a big sister, I guess."

"Yeah. Well, listen, go back to sleep. I'll let myself out and lock up. I didn't mean to wake you, I just wanted you to know that if you want me to drop the case, I understand." I moved toward the door.

"Wait," Marcie said. She rearranged her pillows and worked herself into a sitting position, back propped against pillows propped against headboard. She pulled the sheet to her neck. "I'm not asleep yet, really. I took something about half an hour ago and it's made me fuzzy. But don't go yet, I want to talk about this some more."

I went back over and sat on the edge of her bed. Heat from her leg, resting lightly against the small of my back, flowed through the sheet. I shivered.

"I was thinking 'bout what you said . . . blackmail," Marcie managed stupidly. "Maybe Copel," she yawned mightily. "Sorry. I mean, maybe Copel took those pictures and planted the stuff in Eddie's place."

It was an interesting angle. "Why?"

Another yawn. She shook her head at the end of the yawn. "Lord, why doesn't this stuff ever work when you *want* to sleep?" In the dark, I smiled. "I don't know why," she continued. "Maybe because he was in trouble—with these Mafia people, maybe. He stashed the stuff at Eddie's, where no one'd look for it." She stretched, working off the sleeping pill. Already her speech was clearer.

"Well," I said decisively, "that's certainly something to think about."

"Then think about it, will you? Because I still don't believe my brother has anything to do with this . . . this other stuff."

"You may be right." But I doubted it, doubted it seriously, if only because what I had found at Bell's place wasn't hidden away, just stored away. Yes, Copel had had a key to Bell's place and it was a natural spot to hide something if he was looking to hide it— from, say, the Mob. But it just didn't feel right, even if I didn't say so to Marcie. Instead I yawned, so hard my ears popped. "Anyhow, I'd better get going. It has been a long day."

"Not yet." Suddenly she folded herself over and was in my arms, holding me tight, very tight and very warm. A little furnace. "Just hold me," she whispered in the cool dark. "I'm scared, scared for Eddie, because of what might've happened to him and because I've never been scared for him before." She held me even tighter, which I wouldn't've thought possible. "He can't really be dead, can he?"

"Nobody knows, Marcie," I said, trying to be consoling and yet honest. I didn't like the way things were going, the way I was starting to feel. I put my arms around her to hold her as she had asked, and only then, when my hand slid up the long uninterrupted stretch of skin on her back, did I know she was naked.

Her own hand was on the inside of my leg, moving slowly, caressingly, upward until it found the part of me that had already begun to respond. The caress grew insistent.

"Marcie, I don't—"

And her lips were on mine, her tongue probing deeply. I tasted the mint of her toothpaste, smelled the musky, subliminal scent of her, thought of every good reason to call this to a halt, ignored each of them.

I peeled the sheet from between us and cupped one smooth, full breast. My finger caught the chain looped around her neck and it pulled away. "Damn clasp," she murmured dreamily, and plucked the necklace from her moist skin. She laid it on the night stand but I heard it slither serpentine over the edge to land silently in the carpet. She ignored it. I mauled her breasts. She caught her breath in my mouth and pushed against my hands. Her own hands worked off my coat and began on the buttons of my shirt. When it was gone I lowered her onto the bed, worked my lips against her mouth, my pelvis against hers.

Her fingers slid down my back, scratching lightly, and downward. I fumbled with buckles and zipper, then shed the last of my clothing like a snake leaving behind its skin. Her nails clawed me as I threw the sheet from the bed. Her skin was gray in the blue light. She was slender, rather small for her full breasts. I stroked them again, feeling the hard tips against my palms. She shuddered and dug deeper into my backside with her nails. I kissed her, hard. She sucked my tongue into her mouth with surprising force. Presently, and with some difficulty, I extracted it. "Shall I give you something else to do that with?"

In the darkness I felt her shake her head. "That's not what I want."

"It isn't?" I whispered innocently. "Then what?"

Her fingers gripped tighter and pulled me against her, onto her. She ground her hips against me, at the same time using her tongue on my lips. "Now," she insisted.

"You."

She groaned and reached for me, guided me faultlessly into hot softness.

"Now, you son of a bitch," she breathed feverishly into my ear.

Well, since she asked so nicely . . .

By 1:15 I was on the street, wiping moisture from the back window of the red beast with my handkerchief. It had to be eighty degrees still. A corona of humidity encircled the street lamps. Upstairs, Marcie slept soundly away.

I envied her that.

Behind the wheel I sat momentarily and thought. Not, surprisingly, about Marcie and the wholly unexpected scene that had transpired upstairs. That deserved thinking about, to be sure—the handsome, hard-boiled, cynical P.I. bedding his beautiful, quiveringly available young client may be requisite in crime novels and TV series, but it was unique to my experience. Maybe if it hadn't been I wouldn't be looking to get out of the business.

Which was neither here nor here. What my head worried now was the new angle on the case that Marcie had presented. In my gut I knew when she had said it it wasn't right, but that seldom is enough for my head, which now reminded me that Adrian had failed to recognize Copel's name—which, if he had been her blackmailer/photographer, I would have expected her to know. And OPD did have knowledge of Bell's photographic endeavors, while no such charge had been made or proven against Copel. Also, it seemed to me not quite up Copel's alley—too much work involved for too little money. Blackmail Copel would tackle, but not pornographing. More important, there was no reason to think, no evidence to suggest, Copel was the photographer, therefore no cause to treat Marcie's speculation as anything but that.

I shifted on the vinyl seat. My ass stung where she had dug in her nails when she came. I started the car, directed it away from the freeway and toward Center Street. At that time of night, with little traffic on the streets, the freeway would be no faster. Besides,

I still had some thinking that needed to get done, and that's easier at thirty-five miles an hour than at fifty-five.

My equation was still a distance removed from producing a quotient. As I followed the darkened and deserted streets I tried to make a mental list of what I knew. It was a quick task: Copel was dead, Copel had pictures of Adrian Mallory, Adrian refused to discuss the pictures; Eddie Bell was missing, Bell took the pictures of Adrian, Copel was investigating Bell's disappearance when he was killed.

Pretty depressing, isn't it? The rest of what I "knew" I didn't know for fact—that Bell was dead, dead at the hands of an insane mobster who had killed Copel, too; that Bell and/or Copel blackmailed Adrian and/or her father, Senator Mallory, and/or were preparing to; that more pictures of Adrian were floating around somewhere. These were merely assumptions, maybe good ones, but assumptions nonetheless. You can't build a case on them. And you surely can't come to the truth through them.

My journey was finished before my ruminations were. I detoured, taking Center to Saddle Creek, which merged with the Radial just south of my place; followed the Radial past home sweet home and to the point where it veered off onto Fontenelle Boulevard. I took Fontenelle north, through the park, then circled around, via Ames Avenue and Thirty-first Street, toward my neighborhood, reveling in the night and my solitude, letting warm darkness blanket me and muffle the sounds of my own brain.

It was along Hamilton Street, in a crumbling block east of the Radial, perhaps two, three miles from my place, that I noticed the sign. It wasn't old, but it had a rock-sized piece knocked out of the center of it, where a maroon-and-white Dr Pepper emblem had once been. Below the emblem, in a white rectangle, black letters spelled out the name of the establishment it fronted: George's Car Barn.

I turned the Chevy's protesting tires toward the littered curb across the street from the building, which looked to be a pre-Depression filling station converted to a garage. George's Car Barn would be shortened in conversation to George's Barn, I decided.

In a quickly scribbled note to yourself it could easily emerge as GEO BAR, the final letter lost in hastiness.

Killing the engine I swiveled my head around to inspect the rest of the block. It had all slid pretty far downhill. Most of the buildings, like George's, probably began life in other incarnation—a dry cleaner looked like an old Phillips 66 station, a used-furniture store like a grocery. No telling how many businesses George's building had held over the years. Or how many it would in the future, for George seemed to have gone bust. Words to that effect were drippingly whitewashed over the inside of a large window in the south corner of the building. Several other places along the street had faced similar economic trials. A sign of the recessed times. Here it was like a ghost town—an image I decided wasn't too inaccurate, and one that would appeal to someone needing a little privacy while extracting information from less than cooperative witnesses.

It was also near enough my apartment for Copel to have traveled the distance the night before—though that he was able to even move at all would forever seem to me a miracle.

I started the car again, drove down the block to the cross-street, and up the alley behind George's.

I got out of the car.

The alley was as quiet as the street in front. It held garbage dumpsters for a couple other buildings that shared the alley, some miscellaneous boxes and other debris, and nothing more. I peeked through flyspecked windows facing the alley. Some light from the street came through the garage's front windows. I made out two pits in the floor, mechanic's pits, from the days before every service station in the land had hydraulic lifts. It was an indication of the neighborhood's long-time economic standing that no one had ever filled in the pits and installed lifts. George's was a quickie oil-change-and-lube spot—at least, had been up until a few weeks or months ago. Now it looked totally deserted.

Apparently, I reminded myself. I strongly believed the place was still used, had been used recently, as recently as last night, when Copel was no doubt interviewed there. I was equally sure that Eddie Bell had had an appointment to meet Crazy Al Manzetti there only a couple weeks ago.

I needed in.

I stepped back from the window. It was composed of several small panes of glass, each perhaps six-by-eight inches. It, and the steel back door, were firmly buttoned down.

From the trunk of the red Chevy I took a quart of Quaker State; the owner of a car as old as mine finds it prudent to lug some oil around with him. I also grabbed an old newspaper from my windshield-cleaning supply.

I broke into the can with an oil funnel and, folding the tabloid to quarter-size, poured half the 10W40 in a thick layer over the paper. When it was coated, I carefully lifted it by the upper edge and pasted it, oily side in, to one of the rectangular panes near the window's inside crank. It overlapped the peeling wooden frame only a little.

I carefully set the opened can on the floor of the trunk and got out the jack handle. I smacked the lug end of it once—hard—against the oiled paper. The glass under it gave with a dull crunch, and only a shard or two tinkled against the cement floor inside the building. Even in the night's stillness it made about as much noise as some loose change dropping—and attracted one hell of a lot less attention.

When I peeled away the paper, most of the glass came with it. I wrapped the mess in another sheet of newsprint and deposited it and the jack handle in the trunk. From my emergency box—I told you it was an old car—I took an oversized spot lantern. Gently, I closed the trunk lid.

I reached through the broken pane like I was reaching into a lion's mouth, grabbed the window crank and started turning. It was awkward going, and the frame was swollen a bit from humidity, but I got the window open wide enough to hoist myself through, then quickly closed it again.

There was as much air in the garage as on the moon, and what little there was was made practically unfit for breathing by a thick, unidentifiable, sickening stench that imposed itself over decades'

worth of automotive odors and a strong, oily, smoky smell. The
wing-beats of a rather large number of rather large flies trying to
push out window panes provided the only airflow. The smell, as
much as my fear of being caught flagrante delicto, made me re-
solve to hold a very quick search.

As it was, there wasn't much to search. At a glance you saw
that the building was divided into four areas: the garage itself, a
small and doorless office, a narrow washroom whose door stood
open and another room with a closed door. Storeroom, probably.

The garage bay was practically empty. I scanned the spot lamp
over a half-dozen crusty metal drums huddled together against a
pegboard wall on which still hung a utility lamp, an Allen wrench,
a rubber mallet and a tire iron. A Phillips screwdriver rested on
one of the drums that had lids. The drums were empty. A long
workbench lined half of the back wall; it was vacant except for a
large vise bolted to it, and an old, dangerous-looking coffee cup.

I wandered over to the narrow strip of flooring that separated the
mechanics' pits and shined the bright light into them. The pits
themselves were identical: a roomy rectangular hole in which the
mechanic stood to work on the car driven overhead. The only dif-
ference between the two holes was that one had about a quarter-
inch of water in the bottom.

I looked overhead automatically. Two red hoses, one for air,
one for water, hung from the high ceiling. Neither worked.

On the spotted concrete floor near the edge of the pit were several darker gray spots with spiky perimeters: almost-dried water
drops. I followed them over to the drums and, behind the drums,
to a canvas fire hose on a spigot at the base of the wall. The
needle-spray nozzle still bled a dark halo around itself on the floor.

However long George's had been out of business, someone had
indeed been using the facilities, and recently.

With my white beam I followed the drops back to the pit like a
DWI suspect following a tape line. In one corner of the damp hole
I noticed a small white something. I went down the narrow metal
ladder at the head of the pit and got my shoes a little wet.

The white something was the reverse side of a curled piece of

Kodak paper. On the front of it was a photograph, a color snapshot of a young, thin, dark-haired man who glared with opaque pink eyes into the camera. He looked like he was trying to decide whether to slug the Instamatic operator.

He also looked like Marcie Bell.

And then it fell into place like a roulette ball. The fire hose had been used the night before last, when someone put Morris Copel in the pit, where he couldn't avoid the full brunt of the high-pressure spray, where he got soaked before managing to escape and find me—though not before getting shot—and where he lost the photo of Eddie Bell that Marcie had given him.

It was as I would have guessed—but it's so much nicer not having to guess at such things.

It hardly answered all my little questions, though, like who brought Copel to this malodorous place, beat him, hosed him down, ultimately killed him?

And more important—because I could still guess at who had done it—why?

The stench of the place invaded my mind and my stomach, with no benefit to either. Deciding I could be just as confused in the comfort of my own home, I pocketed the soggy photograph and moved quickly to finish casing the joint.

The little office was the room with the big windows facing the street. I had to keep my beam out of the line of dusty panes while I inventoried the room's contents. They were: a scarred wooden desk, no drawers; a swivel chair that matched the desk cigarette burn for cigarette burn; a gray four-drawer file cabinet, empty; an auto-supply house calendar, which hadn't been changed since April, yellowing on the wall. In a corner of the ceiling a glistening web constructed by the Frank Lloyd Wright of arachnids threw back the spotlight's rays. A couple flies made themselves comfy there.

The washroom was a grimy white sink and a stool, a cracked mirror, a dusty half roll of toilet paper and a horsefly family playing a symphony against an overhead slab of beaded glass.

That left only the storeroom. Its door was shut, stuck but not locked. I pushed against it. I pushed harder and it popped with an elephantine squeal.

When it did, that awful, pervasive stink hit me like a steamroller. I clapped my handkerchief over my nose and mouth and, fighting the gag impulse, entered.

The room was a smallish, high-ceilinged square. It held more drums—ten or twelve—large cardboard boxes, smaller, flimsier boxes of the sort parts come in, a broken straight-back chair that rested on its side against the west wall. And flies. The damn things were holding a convention in that stinking room. I swung my lamp at the cloud they formed and, reluctantly, humming angrily, they parted for me.

Except for dust, the boxes were empty. I turned back to the drums, kicking a few of the nearer ones, those that still had lids, to see if they were empty. They echoed back hollowly, deeply. One apparently had an inch or two of liquid in the bottom. One thudded. I shoved at it with my foot. It was heavy. Its lid was tightly in place, but obviously had once been removed. Someone had replaced it crudely but effectively, crimping the edges solidly in place with heavy-duty pliers.

From the garage bay's pegboard wall, I retrieved the mallet and tire iron. In short, sweaty order I gouged a hole in the side of the drum just under the lip of the lid, jammed in the tire iron and heaved with all my weight. The lid folded back four or five inches.

My held breath gave out and I had to inhale. The stench was now literally overpowering. I bent over, face between my knees, until the lightheadedness passed. Then I looked into the drum.

Inside, of course, was Eddie Bell.

He looked like an overripe banana and smelled of feces and rotting meat.

The flies went crazy. This, after all, was what they had come for.

I scrambled to the filthy washroom and threw up into the sink.

The water, when I rinsed my mouth and the sink, tasted of iron, but it was cold and clean. My lips and the tips of my fingers were numb. My empty stomach was still doing barrel rolls. But my mind, crippled by shock though it was, limped gamely along. It decided that Bell had indeed come to this horrible place on the seventh, keeping his mysterious appointment, and had been killed that very night or within a couple of days at the outside, judging by the body's condition. It had to have been at night, when the block's pathetic businesses shut down and the neighborhood was virtually evacuated.

Bell had been sealed in that metal drum for ten long, sultry days. Only the fact that the place was shut up tight had prevented the discovery of the body for this long.

Now, of course, the cops would have to be let in on the flies' secret. On television I'd be expected to keep the body stashed away until the last two minutes of the show, when I would turn the bad guys over to the slack-jawed flatfoots and say, "And all the evidence you need to convict 'em is in a garage on the other side of town. Bring your own No-Pest Strip."

Unfortunately, in the nonvideo world, the slack-jawed flatfoots would, at that point, haul you in along with the base evildoers and give you an opportunity to acquire a new skill, like license-plate manufacture.

However, I knew that marching into Ben Oberon's office with the announcement that I'd turned up yet another body while butting into the case he'd ordered me only a few hours earlier to butt out of was only a little more advisable than knocking back a cup of rat poison with breakfast. The compromise course was to let some civic-minded but anonymous citizen with outraged olfactories dial 911. The cops would investigate the stench, which in short order would permeate the neighborhood, and the body would be "discovered." In order to guarantee that happy outcome, I'd volunteer to be the citizen myself.

Unthrilled with the prospect of going back for another look at the decomposing Bell, I easily convinced myself that his killer must have removed anything of any importance from his person. I left him to the flies, moved quickly, nervously, through the garage, wiping with a fat wad of toilet paper anything I'd touched that seemed likely to take fingerprints. That meant reclaiming the tire iron and mallet from the storeroom, but I didn't peek into Bell's final resting place.

That done, I let myself out into the alley by way of the metal door, which I conscientiously locked behind me, twisting my hand on the doorknob to obliterate my prints. Reading all those detective novels pays off.

I turned back toward the Chevy and barely had time to jump out of my skin before one of two gigantic men smashed a granite fist loaded with a pistol butt into the left side of my face, sending constellations through my brain, sending me crashing, unconscious, to the oily grit of the alley.

In the dream were giants. **7** After all, I seemed to be meeting up with an awful lot of them; and in this dream, while nothing of any great significance resulted from the meetings, I was painfully aware of the discrepancies in size and weight and strength. It would be, my dream-self determined, far less humiliating to be pummeled by a giant than to have a giant refrain from pummeling you because he knew he could, easily, effortlessly, if he wanted to.

To my dream-self it made a lot of sense.

Painfully, I dragged myself half out of the dream. The wakeful part of me was aware of pain and blackness, and of a red light somewhere above me. Like a darkroom, the dreaming part decided. The whole case was tied to the image—literally, as in the darkroom where Bell processed Adrian Mallory's nude photos; figuratively, in the sense that I seemed prohibited from examining anything in clear, white light.

I was awake, solidly. I knew because now my head throbbed

unmercifully, because now I knew the red light in the darkness was the hot end of a cigar in the mouth of a man standing over me, because now I realized I was again in the garage, lying in one of the mechanics' pits, the dry one. And because now I understood what had nettled me in Bell's apartment, what gave me the uncomfortable sensation of something—something very obvious—being amiss.

There was no developing or printing equipment of any kind in Bell's room, and certainly not enough space to assemble even a makeshift darkroom there.

The photographs—Adrian's and the others—weren't the sort that you leave off at the local Rexall and come pick up next Tuesday. Bell either had a darkroom set up someplace else, or he had been working with someone who had one.

Copel?

I still wasn't inclined to think so, but there was no denying he fit into the equation somewhere. Maybe he was a kind of silent partner of Bell's. It would have to be figured in there somewhere.

Meanwhile, there were other problems to figure out. Namely, mine.

I focused in fairly well on the face behind the cigar. It meant nothing to me. It was just a face, a square face running to plump, on top of a long and solid body.

I dragged myself to a sitting position on the concrete floor. This wasn't as easy as it may sound. My head felt like a rotting zucchini ready to split. I reached up and gingerly stroked the damaged skin. A little blood came away, but it seemed mostly dried by now. I canted my watch toward the paltry light and read the time: 2:45. It seemed reasonable to guess I'd been out for twenty minutes to half an hour. Slowly I checked through my pockets. Everything was in its proper place, but I knew with a kind of chilling certainty that I'd been carefully searched. It didn't matter, there was nothing on me to be found, but I still didn't like it or the vulnerable feeling it left me.

A wave of nausea took hold of me. I fought it, but I'd've probably lost if I hadn't emptied my stomach of everything less than an

hour earlier. Thank heaven for small favors. Across the back of
my mind flitted the observation that I could no longer smell Bell's
rotting corpse, even though the air I breathed was redolent with it.
The nose tires easily. I put the thought out of my head before it
reached my stomach.

"He's up," Cigar said. On the horizon appeared another man,
similarly constructed, a balding giant with a mustache.

"That's swell," said Mustache unemotionally. "We plant ourselves in front of his crummy apartment and sweat like pigs all
fucking day, and then he walks right into our arms when we ain't
even looking for him." He snorted. "What about the boss?"

"He's on his way," Cigar said.

"That's swell," Mustache repeated, and went back to whatever
he was doing, back out of my line of sight. Cigar went on smoking
and staring at me as if I were a television set. I couldn't think of
any good conversational gambits and I had the feeling he wasn't
much of a talker anyway, so I ignored him, closed my eyes against
another onslaught of illness, leaned my head against the stone wall
of the pit.

The boss. Manzetti, of course. Crazy Al, homicidal hoodlum. It
occurred to me that I was in the same position—literally, quite
literally—as Bell and Copel had been in, and look what they had
to show for it. The realization didn't set my mind or stomach at
ease, but it did whisk the last mists out of my head and set my
little gray cells, as Hercule Poirot put it, to work—furiously.

Creative-writing time, class. What was the connection between
Bell and Manzetti? What brought Bell here? What caused Manzetti
to keep Bell from ever leaving?

The photographs. They are the case's common denominator.
Bell had the nude photos of Adrian Mallory, a U.S. senator's
daughter. Never mind for now how he got them, class, the point is
they're great blackmail ammo. Was Bell working for Crazy Al?
No—more likely, Bell was trying to sell the photos to the Mob, as
represented by Manzetti. That worthy organization would be most
interested in the photographs' potential, and would know how to
exploit it to the max.

Wonderful, class. *A* for effort. Now: what happened to trigger Bell's untimely (at least, that was probably his opinion) demise? Two possibilities here: Manzetti double-crossed Bell or Bell double-crossed Manzetti. Or—make that three possibilities, class—both.

Let's say that at least Bell was double-dealing. He withheld some of the photos he was supposed to be selling to Manzetti. What makes me think this, class? Because Copel turns up two weeks after Bell's death with a crotchful of photos of Adrian? Absolutely. Maybe Manzetti realized Bell had double-crossed him, so he killed him. Maybe he was planning to kill Bell all along, and never knew until later he didn't have all the pics. In any event, a couple weeks went by before Manzetti and Copel somehow cross paths. How this happened, boys and girls, remains a mystery. Perhaps Bell and Copel were partners all along, unknown to Manzetti. Perhaps Copel, in Marcie Bell's employ, was looking for the missing Eddie Bell and, as happened to me, got unlucky. Perhaps Copel, in investigating the case, came across the photos of Adrian, recognized her, and decided he could make a killing.

Bad pun, class, and thoroughly unprofessional.

In any event, Copel and Manzetti came together in this place, no more than twenty-four hours ago. Copel was painstakingly worked over, in order to extract from him information, the remaining photos of Adrian or—if Manzetti's reputation was accurate—just for fun. His torturers didn't find the negatives Copel had hid down his pants; he had been around a little. And somehow he managed to break away and drag himself to my place before cashing it in.

Excellent reconstruction, class. Whether it bears any resemblance to actuality, of course, is another matter entirely, but it hangs together well as a strictly speculative equation. Good work. Now, one final question: How does our brave hero extricate himself from the bad guys' clutches and save the day?

Class? *Class?*

Doomed by the bell.

I snapped open my eyes as if rising from a fevered dream. Maybe I was. I'd gone fifteen hours on five hours' sleep, following a nineteen-hour day—which maybe explained the crazy scenario my mind had just run through. Crazy, yes; outlandish, no. It gave me at least the bare bones of a story line to follow. If I lived, perhaps I could upholster them a little.

If I lived. That was problematical. But it was worth pursuing, if I do say so myself. Having had something of a breakthrough concerning the probable course of events in this case, my conceit was now such that I believed I and my razor wit could extricate myself from a situation that two men in the past couple weeks hadn't survived.

On second thought, maybe that wasn't strictly conceit. Maybe it was the only straw I had to glom on to.

Giddy with adrenaline, though still wobbly, I managed to get to my feet—a feat I'd've never managed without a wall to brace against. Cigar had wandered off somewhere, and there was still no sign of Mustache. I started climbing the narrow steel-rod ladder at the head of the pit.

Instantly both giants were at the edge of the hole. "What the heck do you think you're doing?" Cigar demanded from behind the rope burning in his mouth.

I was head and shoulders above floor level when I paused and looked each man squarely in the face. "It's damp down there," I said seriously, trying not to wince at the icy slivers of pain my abused face shot into my brain. "I'll wait for the boss up here, with you." I took another rung on the ladder.

The giants looked at each other. "Wiseass," Mustache decided. He turned back to me and planted a huge wing-tipped shoe on my left shoulder.

I had hoped for this. Clasping the ladder with my left hand, I brought my right up behind Mustache's left knee. I smacked it hard and the knee buckled and collapsed like a folding-chair leg. Mustache cried out in surprise as his considerable weight went to his right foot, the one on my shoulder. I swiveled to the right on the ladder and Mustache toppled over me and into the pit, head-first.

He made an unpleasant sound when he hit. I hoisted myself out of the hole as fast as I could manage and put some distance between me and Cigar, who stared stupidly into the pit. There was no activity there.

"Sebby?" Cigar wondered speculatively into the pit. Then, louder: "Hey, Seb—you okay?"

Nothing from the lower depths. I hoped I hadn't helped Sebby break his neck, but I didn't hope it too hard.

Cigar looked at me. It was a strange look, and didn't seem to belong to that face. The face was used to looking hard and tough and unsympathetic. A trace of jowliness and a slight pouch under the lantern jaw was starting to soften it as its owner gravitated into middle age, but even so it was a tough face. Which is why the wide-eyed look it now gave me—the sort of vacant, wrenching look a kid gets when his first pet makes that unexplainable journey into death—was so out of place.

"Jesus, I think you killed him," Cigar said softly.

I said nothing.

Cigar looked back into the pit. He looked at me, and the wondering expression in his face had evaporated. "Maybe not, though," he said with a verbal shrug. "Okay, look, shamus, we got to get some things straightened out, fast." He started around the edge of the pit, toward me. I had been edging away from him—toward the door, maybe, but mostly away from him. Now I bolted. The workbench was closer than the door. I grabbed from it the tire iron I had used to pry open Bell's crude crypt. It would be about as valuable as dinosaur repellent if Cigar decided to put a bullet through me, but holding it made me feel better.

"Talk from there," I said. I growled it like a B-picture gangster. The idea was to mask the quaver in my voice.

Cigar spread his big hands innocuously. "Fine, it's the same to me. I don't have the time to waste. You neither." He plucked the stogie from his face and tossed it into the other pit, the one with water in the bottom. The hot cigar hissed when it struck.

The hiss was well-timed, for in walked the villain.

Manzetti. Had to be. I was expecting a Robert De Niro type in white suit, Cuban heels, broad-brimmed hat. Maybe a coat laid thoughtlessly over his shoulders. A pencil mustache to complete the picture.

What I got was Rod Steiger in a gray two-piece suit. But it had to be Manzetti.

He was a short man, but built as solid as a fire plug. He was balding. Rather than disguise it, he wore his remaining dark hair close-cropped. His eyes were shiny and dark, like mockingbirds', and heavy-lidded. His mouth was soft, slightly pouting. The entire image was calm, deliberating. An accountant, not a mobster. Crazy Al fit his nickname about as well as a dog fits into a church service.

Following close behind Manzetti was a kid, a tall, reedy kid. You knew the type in school: long and thin, all legs, ears at a ninety-degree angle to the head, Adam's apple that made them look like they had swallowed a billiard ball. This kid—he couldn't've been twenty-two—didn't seem like muscle, but those wiry guys can be deceptive.

There was nothing deceptive about the cannon he pulled from under the front panel of his baseball jacket and leveled at me. "Drop the crowbar," he ordered in what he probably thought was a snarl. "And reach for the ceiling."

I looked at him. "'Reach for the ceiling?' Bug off, sonnyboy, I don't take orders from snotnosed wimps who steal their lines from Quickdraw McGraw. 'Reach for the ceiling,'" I added sarcastically, and the kid looked like he'd been slapped with a fresh mackerel. Brave Nebraska. Fearless Nebraska. Macho Nebraska. Ninety percent USDA choice bull, partly to fool the opposition, partly to fool myself. "Besides," I added carefully, completing the portrait I was painting of the solid P.I. with ice water for blood, "I don't think the boss here wants too many people getting shot up before he knows what those people might know—and who else might know, too." I looked into Manzetti's languid, almost sleepy face. "We don't want a repeat of last night, do we? Very sloppy work."

Manzetti gave no show of emotion, not a flicker. He considered my bravado for a beat, then drawled smoothly, "Put away the gun, Charlie."

Charlie reacted violently again, as if struck—and, in fact, he had been dealt two unexpected blows in quick succession. "But, boss—"

"Goddammit, do as I say!" A quick burst of temper, hot, white and fast, like flash paper, and I gained some insight into the origins of Manzetti's nickname. The kid's cannon disappeared. So did Manzetti's ire, which was as unsettling as its sudden appearance. Now he studied me casually with that same amused, detached look. "You're a brave man," he said quietly. "Or a stupid one."

He turned to Cigar. "So, then, Tom, you had a little trouble?"

"Only a little. He got the jump on Sebby, sent him flying into the pit there. I don't think he's dead, though, 'cause I just heard him moan a little."

Manzetti nodded. "You searched him? He's our man?"

"He's Nebraska, all right, like I told you on the phone. A private license, too, which is something the newspaper didn't say. And he's clean."

The newspaper. I should've realized even the bad guys read until their lips get tired. I should have taken some precautions, made some plans, instead of blundering into their mitts as I had. Been out of the game too long as it is, Nebraska, and the game was never this serious before.

"Clean, huh? He's clean, his place is clean—I suppose that heap out back, too?"

Tom bobbed his head snappily. "Sebby went over it. There was a piece in the glove box, but that's it. No sign of . . ."

Again with the nodding. Manzetti latched his hands behind his back and paced the concrete floor to where I stood. He walked thoughtfully, carefully, as if each step had to be painstakingly planned in advance. Perhaps it did. Manzetti was still a distance from having what he wanted, and two men who could have helped him were dead. As I had said, pretty sloppy. I was counting on his reluctance to repeat the error yet again, with me.

Manzetti stopped mere inches from me. I smelled his aftershave. I didn't care much for it. But he didn't ask my opinion.

Instead, he said, "You realize you're in very serious trouble here." Manzetti, the soul of brotherly concern.

I tried to mimic his tone. "You, too, I think."

He arched an eyebrow in what might have been surprise—mild surprise, mildness seeming to be Crazy Al's alter ego—but he didn't comment on it. Instead: "I believe you have something that belongs to me, something I bought and paid for, something I will have. If you do have it, you'll give it to me. That's right enough. First let's talk about what you're doing here, on private property."

I considered several replies in the course of the next few seconds, and settled on the truth—the modified truth; that seemed to be the only kind I knew lately. "Like the man said, I'm an eye. I was hired to find out what happened to Eddie Bell. That brought me here. As simple as that."

"Who hired you?"

"Someone interested in where Bell got to."

Manzetti made his little half-laugh. "If it's important, you'll tell me." There seemed to be no boast behind this and other statements like it Manzetti made: he simply had never had any reason to doubt the ability of his clout to gain him whatever he wanted. Even now, all the cards seemed to be in his hand, which does tend to give one that air of confidence. "Let's say you tell me about—the Jew . . ."

"Copel," Tom supplied.

"Copel. Tell me about Copel."

I shrugged. "You tell me. You seem to be the last one who . . . spoke with him."

"But you seem to be the guy with all the answers."

"Detective, remember? Deductive reasoning, inductive reasoning—I could never keep them straight. Bell disappears. The man hired to find him is murdered. Word's on the street that you're involved—and there you are. Pretty straightforward stuff, Al."

His face went white on the proper noun, but he recovered quickly. In different circumstances it would have been funny, like watching a recovered alcoholic agonizing over an available bottle, or a reformed gambler fighting an invitation to a "friendly" card game—you know, funny in a sick, sadistic sort of way. In this case, however, there wasn't anything funny about it at all.

"Why did Copel come to you last night?" Manzetti demanded, a little less suavely than had been his style earlier.

"It could have been chance," I said offhandedly. "Probably it wasn't, though. I knew Copel years ago. When you guys let him get away"—I said the words with what I intended to be subtle contempt—"he must've had it in mind to run to the nearest person he knew: me."

"He had something of mine," Manzetti rasped. "Something he had no business having. Something I bought and paid for. I want it back. I want it now."

"You're repeating yourself, Al. And we can't have everything we want, can we? Where would that leave us? Besides, there's a lot of real estate between here and my place. A man can lose things in the dark, especially a dying man."

Manzetti's eyebrows knotted over his eyes. "You're telling me he didn't have anything on him?"

"Actually, I'm telling you no such thing. *Actually,* I'm telling you no thing—nothing, Al, get it?" I like to think I was being as courageous, clever and unflappable as Simon Templar. In fact, I was scared silly, babbling on with nothing in mind beyond clouding the issue as much as I could. Fortunately, it's one of the things I excel at.

If I was looking to spark a reaction, I got it. Manzetti's face underwent a terrible transformation, the worst since Frederic March played Dr. Jekyll. It grew red. It fairly vibrated with pent-up anger. Then it blew in an animal roar, at the end of which was tacked an oath of heroic dimension.

I brought up the tire iron. "Watch it," I snapped. "I'll crack your head like a melon before Howdy Doody here even has time to think about pulling his bazooka." There was Tom the cigar-smoking giant to consider, too, but he seemed strangely absented from the drama.

With effort, Manzetti controlled himself. "You think you're smart, eh?" he spat. "You're not, shamus, you're stupid. Eh?—

stupid. Else you wouldn't fuck with me. You know who I am?''

"Sure I do; you're Crazy Al; I heard of you even before they kicked you out of Chicago.''

Again the face colored, but he worked at it and managed a laugh. Sort of. "That's right, yeah. And you probably know why they call me that.''

"'Cause you're a fun date?''

"That's right, asshole, keep it up. You ever see a man with no kneecaps try to climb a flight of stairs? Ever see a man with busted elbows try to feed himself, or even wipe his own damn nose? Guys who end up like that, they usually start out being funny, you know?'' He glared malevolently. It was like putting WET PAINT on a freshly painted wall—it was a dare.

"Mercy me, yes, I do, Crazy Al. It just shakes me up so. And when I get shooken up I lose things. Like little packages, little keepsakes. No telling where these things end up—downtown, Lincoln, Chicago . . .''

"You better not be playing games with me, asshole.'' He delivered this invective complete with shaking fist, which, I'm sorry, was comical. I laughed.

"Judas priest, Manzetti, I thought they busted you for being crazy, not stupid. I *am* playing games with you, Manzetti, I've been playing games with you since you walked in the door—since Copel dropped dead in my living room, if you want to know the truth of it. And I can keep on playing games with you all night, because you can't touch me. You don't know what I know. You can't kill me—you can't lay a *finger* on me—because you don't know who else might know what I do, or who else might find out if I so much as stub a toe walking out of here. Get it, Al? It's a game all right, a joke, and the joke's on you.'' I reached out and flicked his left ear, the way we used to when we were kids. He grabbed at his stinging ear and, with a kind of strangled roar, turned on his heel and stomped away from me.

Manzetti paced, panting, crazy, like the proverbial crazed tiger. A demon was raging in him, looking to break loose. I wondered if I had pushed it too far, but it was a little late for that now. Finally the man settled on the congregated oil drums not far from us. He attacked them, literally, with fists, feet and elbows. It was an ugly and frightening sight, one that you wanted to run from. It was a little like watching someone else having sex—embarrassing, repulsive and just a little exciting.

When he was finished, his fine suit of clothes was ruined. His hair was a wild mess of spiky strands glued to his sweaty crown. His hands were bruised and bloody. He stood before me, fairly crackling with raw hatred, hunched, disheveled, breathless, burning holes in me with hot eyes. This was one crazy guinea, I decided. He dragged a bleeding hand through the muss of his hair and barked, "Get him out of here."

He was speaking to no one in particular. Tom started, as I'm sure I did; the kid, too, for all I know.

"Al?" Tom ventured.

The anger flared again, but it no longer crackled; a lot had dissipated during his outburst. "You ignorant bastard, I didn't mumble. I said get this fuckhead out of here. Get him out of here, get him out of here, *get him out of here!*" He was on the verge of losing it again. I wondered that something in his head didn't go *blooey*.

The giant he called Tom looked at me expressionlessly and shrugged. "You heard the man. Do it, while you have the chance."

That was good advice. I moved toward the door, trying to keep all three men in sight, maintaining a white-knuckled grip on the tire iron. I was a foot, ten inches, from the door when Manzetti's half-laugh—it, too, weakened by his display—erupted briefly. "What the hell," he said after it. "I can afford to be generous. But only once, shamus." Again he tried valiantly to smooth his hair. "Maybe you know something, maybe you're just blowing smoke. It doesn't matter. Because I've got your number, baby, and you can't pass gas in this town I don't know it. If you have what belongs to me, you can't take it to anybody but me—because if you do it's all over for you." He smoothed his sweaty shirt front with his hands, unaware of the streaks of blood and oil they left, and began to stroll—strut, rather—around the room. Was the brave show for my benefit, the men's, or Manzetti's own?

"The point is," he continued oratorically, growing expansive as his blood pressure declined, "when I buy something I expect to get it. I don't like it being batted all over town like a Ping Pong ball." Circuitously he'd come to within a couple paces of me. "But I tell you what, private eye: I kind of like you. You're short on brains, but you got a lot of balls, and sometimes that's even better."

"You're too kind."

He let it pass. "So here's what I'm going to do: If—*if*—you have what belongs to me, I'm going to ask you to hang on to it for me, just to keep it from getting batted around anymore, understand?"

"We both do, don't we? You don't have any choice in the matter."

"Don't kid yourself," he said flatly. "You must've seen Bell, in the other room?"

I nodded. The recollection turned my stomach.

"Good; keep it in mind. And keep my property good and safe, okay?" He smiled nauseatingly and reached into his pants pocket. "Here." He pulled out a wad of crumpled currency. "Let's say three hundred as a fee for keeping my property safe." I didn't touch the money he proferred. The fifties were old and creased, damp and, in my imagination, unclean. He stuffed them in my shirt pocket. "Everyone deserves to be paid for a job," Manzetti said. Somehow he made it sound like a threat. I let the bills stay where they were. My luck had gone about as far as I wanted to press it—further, in fact, than I could have hoped—so I choked down the inclination to ram the three hundred back down his throat. But I refused to mix his filthy money with my own, as if it would taint that. So it stayed in my shirt pocket. Later, I told myself, I'd go and blow the money on a horse, an idea I think I swiped from a Ross Macdonald novel.

Manzetti pivoted on his tassel loafers, taking in both of his men in the pirouette. It was for them the show was being produced.

Manzetti's face wore a sappy smile, the kind a school kid puts on when he's in trouble but doesn't want his pals to think he's scared. Turn it into a joke. But only Manzetti seemed amused. "Besides," he told his guys, "if he hasn't got it, what the hell do we care about him?"

He laughed—alone—until I said, "That's what I like about you, Al, you're such a graceful loser."

Then I did something I hadn't thought I'd ever do again.

I went out the steel door, climbed into my '73 Impala and drove home.

When I pulled into the stall **8** behind my building and killed the engine, the nerves started.

I sat in the dark, sweating cold perspiration, my hands trembling too violently for me to manipulate the lock button and get out of the car, my innards quivering. I waited it out and after a few minutes, creakingly, left the car and climbed the steel stairs to the second floor.

Three courses of action competed for my attention. In order: leave town and change my name; contact Adrian; contact Marcie.

The telling order in which these options came to mind didn't escape me. Marcie was my client, the one footing the bills, the one for whom I was supposed to be putting forth my efforts. However, I'd gone long past the point where I could keep telling myself I wasn't really more concerned about Adrian's interests. As cynical as I'd like to think I am, there it was. And I couldn't even really tell you why. Because I liked her. Because I felt sorry for her. Because I admired her father, an old friend and political idol. Write your own.

In any event, the first choice was out. I didn't have enough bread to leave town, and I've grown attached to my name, even if it does sound like that of a wild-west hero. When my great-great-grandfather, California bound, had come over from the old country, he rode the rails as far west as his life's savings took him, then called himself after the place fate had carried him to. His descendants were eternally grateful he hadn't decided to homestead in Saskatchewan.

As for the second and third choices—well, it was getting on to four in the blessed A.M., and I just wasn't going to run around town ringing people's doorbells at that uncivilized hour. Marcie, I decided, could surely wait a few more hours before hearing more bad news—the last bad news ever—about her brother. The thought that Adrian could be in some danger traipsed across my sluggish synapses, but I quickly put it aside. If Manzetti had had kidnapping in mind, he could've done it any time, and wouldn't have had to screw around with the pictures. Obviously, abduction wasn't his aim. What he wanted—needed—was those photos. In any event, Adrian would be just as safe or unsafe now as she had been all along.

I liked this line of reasoning. It meant I could go in and go to bed.

Ordinarily I'd've found my way in the dark, but I closed my eyes, put on the lights, and opened them again to survey the damage. Not bad. The place had been searched, but not obviously so. If you weren't looking for it, you might've gone hours before noticing, say, that this closet door that had been closed was now slightly ajar, that that plant was turned the wrong direction, that this lamp shade was out of skew. Nothing dramatic, nothing flung across the room, nothing broken.

I was relieved. Which doesn't mean I liked it at all. But what can you do?

I switched off the lights again, stripped and stepped into a hot shower. Just the thing for a muggy night. The towel was still damp from that morning—yesterday morning, I reminded myself—so, dripping, I went blind into the hall, took another towel from the closet and dried myself while walking the short corridor to the bedroom. I flung the towel in the direction of a chair in the corner, rummaged by touch through a dresser drawer, peeled the spread and top sheet from my bed and stretched out, still without putting a strain on any light bulb.

After my stress-reducing technique I felt almost human again. Ready to sleep, even after everything. I can count on one hand the number of times I've been troubled by insomnia; for me, sleep is an escape. Once I can distract my mind from its overworking, I'm gone.

Of course, sometimes the mind is more cooperative than others. As soon as I closed my eyes, uninvited guests paraded across my inner eyelids. Adrian. Marcie. Jennifer. *Ah, Jen, come to deliver the guilt?* I kicked myself mentally. No cause to blame Jennifer just because my conscience was having second thoughts about my dalliance with Marcie Bell. Of the two of us, Jen was the one who had been totally, consistently honest. It was my idea to clamber aboard the integrity wagon and pat myself on the back for remaining so faithful, so noble, so martyred. And it was I who chose to jump off the wagon—then curse Jen for "making" me feel guilty. Integrity. Right.

I apologize for burdening you with the ethical problems of a sensitive man in the late twentieth century, but they are onerous. Indeed, I must have tossed and turned for all of twenty seconds agonizing over them.

Soon, predictably, my thoughts found other routes to follow, other questions to consider, equations to write. Equations with no quotients at the end. The deeper I delved into things, the deeper and blacker things got. It was like that silly cube toy: every time I turned it in a different direction, I loused up the whole pattern. The only advantage to the cube was that I could put it away when I got sufficiently frustrated.

I began to list everything I didn't know:

How Eddie Bell met Adrian.

How he persuaded her to pose for him; what hold he had over her.

How Marcie could know nothing of her brother's activities, which the police had known of for years.

How Copel knew Bell's game; whether Copel and Bell had been partners.

Where Eddie had his various photographs processed, or where he kept the equipment to do it himself.

How Bell and Manzetti came together.

Why Manzetti was interested in Bell's pictures. (I felt it safe to assume here that the Mob was interested in blackmailing a U.S. senator—though not for mere money—but unless and until I could say for sure, it went on the list.)

Why Bell ended up dead; whether he tried to double-cross Manzetti; whether Manzetti double-crossed him. Or both.

How Copel and Manzetti connected, and all of the same questions surrounding Copel's death.

And so on. The last thing I recall thinking was whether Adrian, if I told her of Bell's demise, would be more open with me, would provide me with answers to some of these questions, or at least new roads to wander. And if, should she still be reluctant, it was time to talk to her father.

Sounded like I was going to tell on her . . .

I slept.

For about ninety minutes. At 5:34, by the digital clock at bedside, I woke. Suddenly and completely, afraid to move, even to breathe. That used to happen to me once or twice a year when I was a kid. It meant I'd been dreaming about werewolves. But that ended when I was about fourteen. Things had gotten a whole lot scarier since then. I lay a full minute in the diffused purple darkness, waiting. Nothing. I heard, and had heard, no sound. And yet I knew with sickening certainty, the left side of my head throbbing in time with my racing pulse, that someone was in the apartment.

Again.

It must have been eighty degrees in that place but I went cold and shivery.

Silently, I slid from the mattress and trod lightly the short hall to the black living room, thinking how similar this was to last night's fun and games. This time, however, instead of a steam iron I carried a revolver taken from the dresser and tucked under my pillow before I said my prayers. Part of my new get-tough policy with unannounced, predawn drop-in guests.

I'd just passed the bathroom door when a pair of iron arms shot out of the blackness and grabbed me. One went round my lower face to keep me from yelling, the other tried to knock the gun from my hand. The first was more successful than the second. We wrestled around a bit while I tried to get the gun in a shooting position and he tried to stop me. At times like this I wish I was one of those huge, solid chunks of meat like Travis McGee or Spenser—six-ten or something, two hundred and fifty pounds, all muscle and bone. Either of those fictional detectives would've had his assailant stacked like kindling by now. Me, I come in an inch or so under six feet, and the only exercise I get is grappling with childproof caps. Being in just my skivvies, I couldn't even give him a good swift kick in the shins. Finally, however, I managed to waltz him backward, off balance, into the bathroom doorjamb, which he hit with a satisfying crack.

In that instant his grip loosened just a notch, but enough for me to duck low, cock my free arm and drive it back elbow-first into his crotch.

Immediately I was released as, with a grunt and a sharp intake of air, my attacker doubled over to tend to his injured privates. I snapped on the light over the mirror and was sort of surprised— sort of not—to find Manzetti's giant gun, the one he called Tom, hunched over on my bathroom floor, half gasping, half retching.

Shaking with exertion, anger and nerves, I patted him down and removed from him a clip-on holster. I tucked his gun under my armpit and shoved my own weapon into his face. "You stupid son of a bitch, I should blow your face off right now. This is my house; the cops wouldn't even look at me funny."

It might as well have been a licorice stick I held to his head for all the attention Tom paid it. He writhed on the floor, clutching his balls, moaning. "I—wasn't going to hurt—you," he croaked with some effort.

"Forgive my paranoia," I growled. "I must be getting jumpy in my old age." I grabbed a fistful of sport coat and yanked a couple of times for emphasis. "Lucky for you I didn't want to have to scrape your brains off my walls in the morning," I yelled. "And that I want you to go back to Manzetti and tell him this is no way to ensure his 'property' doesn't end up where he wouldn't like to see it."

Tom shook his head. His face was an alarming shade of gray and his eyes were tearing but he'd reclaimed some of his wind. "Not—Manzetti—" he rasped hoarsely.

"What?"

He looked up at me. A wince of pain creased his face, but he quit looking like he was going to barf his guts up all over the floor. "Not Manzetti," he repeated. "He didn't send me. If he knew I was here he'd like to shoot me in the balls instead of just elbow me."

"Not a bad idea; I'll have to keep it in mind. All right. If Manzetti didn't send you, what are you doing here?" I mussed up his clothes a little more to show him I meant business. I was getting awfully tired of questions with no answers, of avenues of speculation that ended in cul-de-sacs. I aimed to call a screeching halt to it there and then.

"I—can't say."

I jabbed my gun up below his left shoulder blade. "Try," I growled in my best tough-guy voice.

"I can't. He'd kill me if I said."

"And I'll kill you if you don't." That came from a James Bond movie. "Now or later, Tommy, your decision."

He agonized over it. I prodded him again with the business end of the gun, in case he'd forgotten it was there. "All right, all right," he finally bleated. "Maybe I can smooth it over with him."

"Just turn up that old Neapolitan charm, chum, and I'm sure you'll have him munching out of your mitts in no time. Whoever 'he' is. . . ?"

Tom sighed heavily, like a weight was coming off his chest. Which probably isn't too far off the mark. "I been part of Manzetti's territory—north side—since before he ever came to town. Manzetti, that asshole, he thinks he's running me. Well, he's supposed to be. But he ain't.'' Tom puffed himself up a little—no easy feat when you're crouched over on a bathroom floor—and boasted, "I get my orders straight from Gunnelli."

Gunnelli. The main man, the big boss, the head of the entire Omaha operation, answerable only to and directly to Chicago, for which Omaha is something like a branch office in its gambling and sharking ventures. Small but profitable, very profitable. And rather important, too, disproportionately to its size. Salvatore Gunnelli. Sal the Gun, as the papers had called him thirty or forty years ago, when the papers were big on making up handles like that.

Oberon had called it: I was dog-paddling out pretty far from shore.

I said, "I thought everyone got his orders from Gunnelli." I realized, of course, that Omaha was divided into territories over which lower-level bosses—lieutenants, as the crime novels have it—held sway, but, like division managers in a corporation, the lieutenants, and everybody in the chain of command, reported to Gunnelli—ultimately, to Chicago.

"Don't kid yourself, huh?" said Tom derisively, the color returning to his face, the starch to his backbone. "Everybody works for themselves, just some more than others."

Then that was it: Manzetti was getting a little independent for Gunnelli, who had enlisted Tom to keep an eye on him and report his activities to Gunnelli. I put the question to Tom and got a sullen look that said volumes.

"Now that has some interesting story possibilities," I muttered half aloud.

"Hey, can I get up here?" Tom asked.

I looked around the room. I know you can't tell, because I hide it so well, but I'm a very nervous sort of guy when it comes to the Mafia snooping around my bathroom. "Yeah-h," I said slowly, "but I want you in the tub." He looked at me like I had two heads. "In the tub," I repeated firmly. "Like I said, I'm getting paranoid in my dotage. I want you sitting in the tub—on your hands, too, if you don't mind terribly—so I know you can't pull anything fast and cute."

He shrugged, more with a look than a gesture. "You're the boss."

"I'm glad one of us thinks so."

Tom climbed slowly, painfully, into the tub. It was still wet from my shower, but he didn't complain. I wouldn't have either: he looked too ridiculous, two hundred pounds of gangster, fully clothed, in my pale pink bathtub. Oddly, however, it didn't seem to tickle either of our funny bones.

"Comfy?" I said testily.

"Yeah, yeah."

"Wonderful. Okay, so there's bad blood between Manzetti and Gunnelli. What's it have to do with me?"

"That's what I started to tell you back in the garage, before Manzetti showed up." Tom wagged his dark head. "That's one crazy guinea, you know that. Man's only playing with about half a set of marbles."

"I noticed. Quit stalling." I waggled the gun a little again. "I want the big picture, Tom, so I know where I fit into it."

He looked at me speculatively. The gun didn't bother him that much. I suppose he'd dealt with tougher customers than even me. "Okay, here's the deal," he said after he'd given it some consideration. "I think you and Gunnelli gotta meet."

"You running some sort of underworld lonely hearts' club, or do you have some other intention?"

"Well, I shouldn't even be telling you, not without Gunnelli gives his okay first. But, seeing's how you kind of have the advantage . . . I can probably smooth it with the boss. So look, all it is is that Gunnelli wanted for me to set up a meeting with him and Bell, then with him and Copel. Neither of them happened, like I'm sure you can figure out. But I figure that when I tell him about tonight, I mean you and Manzetti, well, he's gonna want me to set up a meet with you and him."

"And you're getting your ducks in a row early."

"Nah, I'm just trying to get everything set up first. That means I gotta warn you about Manzetti. They don't call him Crazy Al for nothing. That's what I started to tell you back at the garage before he showed up. I was going to tell you to clear out of there before he came—and to *stay* clear of him after."

"What a saint. And I suppose if things got ugly—uglier—you were going to turn into the Incredible Hulk, punch a hole in the wall with your pinky and haul me out of there on your big green back."

He smiled humorlessly. "Hey, I didn't expect you to buy into it right off," he said offhandedly. "But think on this: How do you figure someone in the shape Copel was in got out of that place with four guys—three of them with guns—sitting on him?"

I remembered thinking it had been a miracle Copel even managed to climb over the patio railing. "You."

"Hey, you're in the money, mister. Yeah, it was me. And he'd've made it, too, except Charlie—that pimply kid always sucking up to Manzetti—popped off a lucky shot." He shook his head with something very much like regret, though I found it hard to believe it was for Copel.

"And what accounts for your admirable humanitarianism?"

"Huh?"

"How come you let Copel get away?"

"I told you, 'cause Gunnelli wanted to meet with him. See, he wanted me to arrange this meeting with Bell, but Manzetti queered that all right."

"He killed Bell."

Tom gave me a look that would've melted a bulkhead. "Pal, 'killed' ain't the word for what Manzetti did to that poor sucker. You saw how he lit into those oil drums tonight? Well, that's what he did to the kid, Bell. Jesus, what a mess. Before me and Sebby could even move, that kid was a pile of bloody meat." He grimaced at the memory.

My stomach pitched. "What brought it on?"

"Jeez, I don't think I oughta be tel—"

Again I moved the gun in tight little circles. "Come on, Tom, let's not go through this every two minutes. It's getting redundant. Just pick up the narrative pace, will you; the readers are getting edgy."

He frowned at me. "I thought you were just double-talking Manzetti, trying to confuse him, but that's the way you always talk, ain't it? Okay—well—how much *do* you really know about what was going on back there tonight? I mean, *were* you just blowing sunshine up Al's skirts, or did you know what you were talking about?"

"There was plenty of each going on," I admitted. "Look, if what we're talking about here is the pictures, I know about them. At least, I know enough about them to make things uncomfortable for people if they make things uncomfortable for me." That was tossed in as insurance; things were foggy enough that I couldn't really be sure to whom my words would ultimately be reported.

"Well, I'll be damned," said Tom around a slow, sly, appreciative smile. "I about convinced myself that you were just bullshitting. Okay. Well, a few weeks ago—just before Gunnelli has me start keeping an eye on Manzetti for him—this joker Bell gets in touch with Manzetti, or Manzetti hears about him, or something. I don't exactly know how it works, but they're talking deal pretty soon."

"For the pictures."

"Yeah. So they come up with a figure—and not much of one, neither, 'cause this Bell's about as green as a dollar bill. That's how he wound up dead. See, about a couple weeks ago him and Manzetti are supposed to close the deal. We all meet at the garage—kid didn't even object to that, meeting on Manzetti's turf—him and Manzetti and me and Sebby. And Charlie, of course. We've got a suitcase full of cash, he's got a box of negatives—and pictures, on account of part of the deal's that Manzetti gets *everything* with this governor's daughter or whoever in them. Only there are more pictures than there are negatives." My belly did another loop-de-loop and the effects must've shown on my face, for Tom seemed to notice it. He made a noise with his lips that was something like an unfunny laugh. "Yeah, incredible, ain't it? Sebby goes through the box and comes up with pictures there're no negatives for.

"And, of course, Manzetti blows a gasket 'cause the kid's trying to rip him off. And, like I said, before anyone knows anything he's beaten the kid's brains out with his fists." Which was exactly the wrong thing to do, naturally, because it didn't give Manzetti the missing negatives and it closed off his only access to them—and however many others Bell might have withheld but hadn't been stupid enough to leave prints of in the box.

"So a week, ten days go by," Tom resumed, "and Manzetti gets word from this two-bit named Copel that he has to meet with him about some real important things, lets him know it's about the pictures, I guess, else Manzetti would've told him to get stuffed. They meet at the garage. And they dance around, kind of like you and him did tonight. Copel says he knows about Manzetti and Bell—big deal; that was on the streets the next day—and he can supply the rest of the negatives and stuff. For a hundred grand. Well, Manzetti goes completely apeshit again, starts pounding the hell out of *this* guy. Only me and Sebby are ready for it and we pull them apart before Manzetti does it again." Tom pulled a face. "Talk about never learning, huh?"

"Well, you know what Santayana said about those who cannot remember the past being condemned to repeat it."

"No, what'd he say?"

Sometimes I don't know why I even bother. "I'll tell you some other time. So you managed to peel Manzetti off of Copel . . ."

"Yeah, yeah. And when he cools down, of course, he knows that he can't afford to kill Copel, too. Shit, we've got his first mistake stinking up the other room—'cause the river's too low to sink it—and he's about to do the same thing over again. Asshole." According to Tom, it was Sebby's grand idea to put Copel in one of the mechanics' pits and use a high-pressure needle-jet hose to blast the location of the missing negatives out of him. I decided Tom wouldn't appreciate the irony of Copel having those negatives stuck down his pants the whole time, so I didn't share that nugget of information with him. When the hose didn't work, Manzetti ordered them to drag Copel, soaking wet and half conscious, from the pit and bring him to the workbench. There, one by one, each of his fingers would be put to the vise until he begged to tell them where he had the negatives.

Before Copel had to endure that, Tom created the distraction that allowed him to escape.

"When Manzetti and him were wrestling, I threw my cigar into those drums. I figured there was enough oil and grease and crap in there to make a little smoke, at least. I guess it must've smoldered a while, then it flared up real good. Yeah, it's too bad Copel didn't make it." Tom was silent a half-minute or so. I was touched by his sensitive contemplation of Morris Copel's untimely passing, until he said, "Hey, is it okay if I smoke?"

"Hey, only if you catch fire." His mouth turned downward sourly but he accepted it like a stoic otherwise. I took advantage of his somewhat sullen silence to do some thinking. For one brief, shining moment it appeared that everything was making sense, fitting together beautifully. But, on closer inspection, it was apparent the pieces had gaps between them.

For instance: I knew what Manzetti wanted the photos for. His object could be nothing other than blackmail, and for nothing so mundane as money. No, the photos of Adrian were meant to put Daniel G. Mallory in Manzetti's hip pocket, for which Chicago would kiss him. It would also tend to discredit Gunnelli, who was already having to contend with factions, here and in Chicago, that believed Sal the Gun was getting too old for the job. That, plus Manzetti's friends back in Chicago—the ones who, according to Oberon, fixed it so Manzetti was merely demoted, not ousted— would ensure Crazy Al virtual carte blanche. And it didn't take more imagination than I possessed to guess what Manzetti would demand: Omaha. He'd still be stuck in the sticks, but at least he'd be in *charge* of the sticks.

I liked it. It tended to explain a lot, up to and including why Gunnelli might want to see me—or Copel, or Bell, or anyone with access to the remaining pictures. What it didn't explain was why Manzetti had his underwear in such a wad over getting a hold of the missing negatives. After all, a blackmail victim doesn't care whether he's being bled with twenty, forty or two hundred photos.

Surely what Manzetti already had in hand from his fatal dealing with Bell was plenty of leverage over Mallory, if he chose to use it. That he had waited—and had worked himself into a lather over collecting a complete set—didn't make sense. At least, not to me; I was certain Manzetti had his reasons. They called him Crazy Al, but he was also crazy like a fox. That's how he'd lived so long, how he'd survived the debacle in Chicago. He had a reason, all right.

And then there was Gunnelli. He wanted to get a hold of some of the same sort of pictures Manzetti had, but what did he hope to gain? Manzetti was already ahead of him there. Why didn't Gunnelli move to shut Manzetti down while Crazy Al hesitated, waiting for the rest of the pictures? As head of the Omaha territory, Gunnelli certainly must have had the power. Or were Manzetti's Chicago friends powerful enough to frighten even Sal the Gun? So powerful they prevented Gunnelli from taking steps to ward off the power struggle taking place, or about to take place, in Omaha?

I studied my visitor. He was shifting uncomfortably in the tub and casting furtive sparks my direction. Maybe I could have plied him with my artful questions, but I doubted it would yield much. He was pretty small potatoes, when you came down to it. Gunnelli had probably elected to make Tom his undercover agent because Tom was so thick and unimaginative, too much so to harbor any ambitions of his own—which made him immune to Manzetti, because the realization of people's ambitions is the first incentive an empire-builder offers; at least, one who knows how to build. Tom possessed a certain innate shrewdness, a certain cleverness, that would make him a good observer and a perfect spy, but it didn't run deep enough to make him any kind of a judge of what transpired below the surface of what he observed.

Besides, start at the top is my motto.

"Okay, Tommy, let's go see the man."

"Huh? Gunnelli? Are you kidding? The sun ain't even up yet. Besides, I haven't told him you're coming."

"Just when I had my heart all set on it. All right, then, you go make the appointment or whatever it takes; I'll wait here until I get your call. What's the matter, Thomas, you look all troubled."

"I think I better stay with you. You made Manzetti look like a real jackass tonight. This time I'm gonna make sure Gunnelli gets to see his man before Crazy Al knocks him off."

"Your concern for my well-being is truly heartwarming, but forget it. In the first place, even Manzetti has enough brains to realize he has to keep his hands off me, because he doesn't know where his precious pictures might end up if anything happens to me." One of my little signals went off in the back of my noggin, but I didn't have time to answer it now. I ignored it and hoped without much hope that I'd be able to pick up the thread later. "And in the second place," I added distractedly, "my Murphy bed's at the cleaner's, and you're certainly not sleeping in my bed. And so, though I know it'll blow my Michelin rating, I'm going to ask you to—how can I put this delicately?—blow."

Another mouthful of protests began. I hefted the gun and put a stern look on my face. "Okay, then, I'll give you a choice. You can sleep at home or sleep here—permanently." He must've known I was bluffing but he acquiesced anyway. Slowly, cautiously, we marched to the door, me with two guns pointed at the small of his back, him with two hands raised half-assedly toward the ceiling.

I had the door three-quarters shut behind him before the light went on and he turned back. "Hey, what about my gun?"

"Oh, sorry, the management isn't responsible for lost articles. Only prepositions and pronouns."

"Huh?" he said, but I shut and locked the door on it.

At 8:30 the alarm bleated at **9** me. I stabbed it with my finger and lay motionless for five minutes, proving to myself that no amount or force of wishing would turn back the hands of time, or the liquid crystal displays of time, before dragging myself upright.

I felt like hell, and I don't think I can add anything to those four words. A return to Nodland was definitely an attractive proposition, but my friend Tom had already called to tell me I had a 10:00 appointment with Sal Gunnelli. Duty called. Unenthusiastically I began the ritual: started water boiling, showered, shaved, made coffee, drank same, dressed and was on the road by 9:05. Not too noteworthy, unless you take into account that I managed it all without waking up.

Burt Street on a weekday at that hour is deserted. I took it toward the river to Sixteenth, then down to South O, a tattered but comfortable neighborhood built by immigrants, mainly Poles and Italians, and peopled by their second- and third- and fourth-generation descendants. Off of Sixteenth and Vinton is a drugstore, a corner drugstore, that doesn't think it's a supermarket or a sporting-goods store or a department store. It's a hole-in-the-crumbling-wall, smaller than some caskets, almost totally given over to an old soda fountain complete with round stools with cracked vinyl seats. There's a comic book rack in the back—purposely near the prescription counter—and a resident horde of kids who have it confused with the public library, surrounding it like Indians surrounding settlers in a B western.

"Hey! You gonna read 'em or buy 'em?" The sound from behind the prescription desk could be duplicated by dragging a file over iron.

"Read 'em," admitted a twelve-year-old voice.

A lifetime ago I would've been the wiseass kid, and Carmine Costello the raspy voice of authority. Now the voice was Costello's son, Pat, and I was whatever I was.

"Maybe you should just rent them out, Pat," I suggested.

A dark eye, looking something like the last ripe olive in the jar, rolled in my direction. "You! You're a fine one to talk. For three years when I was a kid my only job was to shoo you out of this store. Now you're back tellin' me how to run it." He looked back over at the kids, who hadn't budged, and shrugged philosophically. "Aw, maybe you're right." He grinned big ivory teeth. "Be right with you."

Pat went back to filling his prescription and I went over to the fountain. One of Pat's innumerable kids brought me a cherry cola. Two high-school-age girls, one fat, one skinny, were my only company when Pat's kid went to tend something else in the shop. The girls ignored me. The skinny one ate a banana split. At nine in the morning, a banana split. The fat one watched her as if she were watching someone make love.

Pat came over. He looked the same as always: thick black hair brushed up and back like Elvis's; olive skin; long, narrow face; pharmacist's white smock. He placed his wiry, six-foot self on a stool next to me and eyed me affectionately.

"Where you been hiding out?"

"Business has been good. The writing biz. It keeps you busy if you're trying to make a living at it."

Pat nodded, his face solemn, his shiny eyes laughing. They were deep-set and surrounded by a network of crow's feet that provided him a permanent squint. "But it's not the writing biz that brings you back to the old neighborhood."

"Do you imply that I'm obvious?" I gave him the film I took from Eddie Bell's camera. "Give this a bath for me, will you? I don't need prints. The end of it'll be blank; that's okay."

Pat made a noise. For someone like him—a fairly well accomplished amateur photographer of the school that holds that the photographer's job only *begins* when he snaps the photo—the simple task of developing a 35mm roll was next to nothing. He dropped the cylinder in a side pocket of his smock. "You need it now? I can have Freddie watch the store—"

I waved a hand. "No huge rush. Besides, I gotta split quick. Important business meeting, you know. Anyhow, I have a feeling I already know what's on that roll, and it probably doesn't matter much. I just like to run everything down."

"I thought you said it was the *writing* business that's been good."

"Well—not that good. And you gotta eat."

"Speaking of which, when're you coming over for dinner? Angela, every day: 'When you gonna ask him over, when you gonna ask him over?' But I never see you. I tell you, you're wrecking my marriage.''

"Good, then it's working. I always said Angela was too good for you.''

"And I always agreed. But it's only fair to warn you, you steal her away and you have to take all seven kids, too.''

"And I thought *I'd* been busy.''

We had a good laugh over our wonderful wittiness, then I slipped Pat another package, a large gray envelope, the type I mail out manuscripts in. "And hang onto this for me, too, huh?''

He took it, saw it was sealed tight, and said, "Sure. What's in it?''

"My memoirs,'' I said. It wasn't too far off: It contained a stream-of-consciousness report of what had been going on since Copel dropped in on me, my knowledge and my speculations, names, locations, everything. I sat up for an hour after throwing Tom out of my place, typing it out. I'd been bluffing, after all, with pictures that would end up ''in the wrong hands'' if anything befell me; if someone decided to call that bluff, I thought it'd be some small consolation that this opus would reach Oberon. "If,'' I said slowly, "I'm not back for it in—oh—a couple days or so, why don't you open it. Inside there's an address I'd like you to get it to.''

Pat nodded solemnly. "Uh-huh. I'll put it in the safe.'' His face was screwed up in a look of extreme concern. "It's something big, isn't it? I mean, just look at you. Your eyes are red, your face looks like an eggplant. You look like death warmed over.''

I stroked the bruise along the left side of my face. Gingerly. "There's been some improvement then.'' I drained the cola glass. "Yeah, it's something big, I guess. I don't know. I haven't gotten a good look at it yet. At least, not all of it.'' I stood. "Gotta run, Pat. I'm due in Regency in about half an hour. If you can run the pictures tonight, I'd appreciate it.''

"Sure, sure.''

I squeezed his shoulder. "Look, I appreciate the concern. But don't worry about me. I look worse than I really am, mainly because I've had only about ten hours' sleep in the past two days." I tweaked his khaki-colored cheek, because he hated it. "You worry too much, Pat, you always did."

"Only over people who need worrying over. You and my fifteen year old." He patted the film roll in his pocket. "What should I expect?"

I glanced over toward the girls, who were too wrapped up in whatever girls get wrapped up in to notice a couple old guys like Pat and me. "Naked ladies."

Pat's black eyebrows climbed dramatically. "I'm shocked. What would your mother say?"

"I'm not worried; I'm not the one whose mother lives with him."

"Mother-in-law," Pat corrected, "but good point." He held a finger to his lips. "Discretion."

"Your middle name. Also, there's a client in this, so I can reimburse you for your trouble."

"And that never hurts," said Pat, though we both knew he'd do it for nothing. He had, plenty of times. When I was in the game full-time I always took this sort of business to Pat—though ordinarily I knew what was on the film, having exposed it myself in the course of, typically, a divorce case—because Pat was good, and fast, and knew how to keep his mouth shut, and didn't cry if I wasn't able to slip him anything this time. He knew I'd make it up next time or the time after, when the client was fatter. It had always been like that. As the saying goes, Pat and I go back a long ways.

Which is why I felt bad. I used to see Pat, and Angela and Mama and the kids, fairly often in those old days. Less so, much less so, now—this was maybe the second time since New Year's, and both times were because I needed a favor out of Pat. It was uncomfortably exploitative. More so because I couldn't stay now.

As usual, Pat said nothing. He was the most understanding man on the planet. I always hated that about him.

On the sidewalk I took a deep drag of muggy air in an effort to clear my head of the dust that had collected there. Immediately I was taken back to childhood, the way some odors can do more sharply than any image. The world today smelled exactly like a turtle bowl I had when I was a kid. The sky was a funny bluish gray overcast, close enough to touch, not cloudy but certainly not sunny. It was hard on the eyes, but since I hadn't gotten around to replacing the sunglasses I sat on in the car the week before, I had to rough it on the freeway. Near the drugstore I got on I–480 south, at the point it becomes westbound I–80. That skirts the extreme south of Omaha, and links up with I–680, which runs north-south on the west edge of town. At Dodge Street I got off the freeway, looped the cloverleaf and ended up in Regency.

Regency's one of those tony developments of sprawling brick-faced ranch-style houses spaced well apart, fake-looking but real lawns, circular driveways and circular streets that don't seem to go anywhere but around and around. Fortunately the development is less than a mile square, so eventually you're bound to stumble across your destination.

Eventually I stumbled across my destination. A real effort was called for to keep me from just driving past it and away. From everything. The days when I could get by on a couple hours' sleep a night were long since gone, and from the way my head dully throbbed a reggae beat, the way my insides felt unattached to anything, I knew my interpersonal communications skills wouldn't be up to their usual stratospheric standards. In other words, I felt crappy, and when I feel crappy I tend to forget to edit my off-the-cuff remarks.

But there I was. The house was a low-slung earth-toned number. Large? Well, if you were going from one end to the other you'd be well-advised to pack a lunch. The lawn was as green as a pool table, and as smooth. A brick wall the color of the house kept the yard from running into the street. Near the gate, a small brown box hung on the brickwork. I got out of the car and opened the box. Inside was a phone with no dial. I lifted the receiver and it rang through automatically, answered by a woman's voice with a curiously precise lilt. She activated the gate electronically from somewhere in the house when I identified myself. The gate shut behind me after I drove through.

Sometime before Christmas I reached the top of the elliptical drive, where the house lay like a high-rise on its side. A petite young woman stood, dwarfed, between the fat white doric columns that supported the roof over the entrance. The woman's hair was the color of sunset, her face a lighter shade of gold. She was small-boned, classically attractive, appealing in a cool, refined way as opposed to, say, Marcie Bell's electrical sexiness. She wore a pale blue suit, the jacket of which was cut along the lines of a sleeved vest. Under it was a cream-colored blouse, open at the neck. Little jewelry. Heels high but not ludicrously so. The "dress for success" guys would've approved.

She came briskly to the driver's side of the car and introduced herself as Helen Tosco. Helen Tosco's eyes were unusually dark, I thought, for a woman of her coloring, and they shone like black stars. She invited me to park the machine anywhere along the drive. I could've parked fifty there.

We entered the house. It was quiet and cool, decorated in a very simple, even sparse fashion that, I gathered from magazines, was the style. "You're right on time," she told me as I followed her through a foyer with genuine tile on the floor and genuine wood on the walls, through a living room with sea blue carpet on the floor and attractive, anonymous watercolors on the wall, and through a dining room with hardwood on the floor and floor-to-ceiling windows on two of the four walls. "Mr. Gunnelli is waiting on the patio," she said. That was through a set of glass doors off the dining room. By the time we got there I was winded.

Gunnelli was in his late seventies, I knew, but he looked twice that. He was thin—emaciated—and pale, his skin a yellowed, waxen mask stretched taut over the bone, crisscrossed with more lines than a Rand McNally atlas. His eyes, once no doubt blue, were watery, colorless, empty-looking—like a dog's eyes at night when the light catches them just so. His hair was a soft white fleece on the sides and back of his head. His hands were claws, and they held, shakily, the *Wall Street Journal*. He sat under a sun umbrella at one of those white wrought-iron tables that are usually aluminum. This one was the genuine article.

Gunnelli appeared not to notice us until the woman spoke. "Mr.

Gunnelli, this is Mr. Nebraska, the gentleman Tom Carra told you about.'' The old man looked up from the news capsules on page one and nodded. His thin stiff lips peeled away from shiny yellow teeth in what I took to be a smile. I've seen more appealing grins on iodine bottles. He set aside the paper and waved his trembling hand in invitation. Helen Tosco pulled out a metal chair for me and I sat. I'd expected her to silently vanish after the introductions—the Mob not being noted for its equal-opportunity efforts—but to my surprise she took the next chair over and seated herself.

The old man stared at me, through me, with those vacant eyes. For a dreadful instant I thought the man must be a feeb, the woman his nursemaid/interpreter, which would make for a fun conversation. However he soon shifted his gaze past me and toward the house. His lips parted in the false start old people sometimes make in speaking, then bellowed to the house, "Jimmy! Coffee!'' The voice was a deep bass bullhorn that needed no amplification to be heard inside through the closed doors. I wondered where in the fragile old frame he stored it, as well the energy to put behind it.

He returned his eyes to my face. I got another death's-head grin and felt a trickle of sweat run down my left side. He was a spooky old bird. "Thank you for coming,'' he rumbled deeply, which set my unsteady innards vibrating. "Forgive me for not standing.'' He slapped a leg. "I cannot always depend on these old pegs.'' Sixty years in this country—and, I didn't doubt, sheer determination—had scoured from his voice any trace of accent, leaving only the careful, meticulous enunciation of someone for whom English is not the native tongue. The woman had the same precision of speech, but with someone her age I'd've bet it was drummed into her head over several years' worth of English lessons.

Gunnelli eyed me warmly—as warmly as the icy eyes could manage anymore—like the prodigal son. "I am so glad we have this chance to meet,'' he said.

"It was an offer I couldn't refuse.''

It was also a stupid-ass thing to say, given whom I was saying it to; besides, it was inaccurate: our scene was as much like *The Godfather* as *Old Yeller*. I was a little disappointed, in fact.

The Tosco woman, meanwhile, shot darts at me with her black eyes as Gunnelli roared in apparently sincere laughter. "Very good, very good," he croaked as a tear escaped down the right side of his creased face. "And I'm glad you thought so, too; horses are much too expensive and beautiful to be cutting off their heads and leaving them among people's sheets."

Smiling lamely, I ran my palms along my thighs. Now that I'd broken the ice by saying something cloddish, it seemed time to get the festivities underway. "Well," I began with stunning originality, "your man Tom—Carra?—said he thought you'd like to have this little chat with me."

He waved it off. "And so I would. But food and business do not mix." He indicated a young, slender man letting himself out of the house. "Here comes Jimmy with our coffee. Then we will have breakfast, and *then* we can discuss our business." He looked at me questioningly.

I figured his opinion of me was rapidly on the way to solidifying already, so I had few points to lose by being tactlessly honest. "To be perfectly blunt, I was hoping we could kind of just get it over with. Maybe I wouldn't ordinarily mind sitting here shooting the breeze for an hour, talking about the weather, the elections, the price of pasta and everything else but what we're here to discuss, but I've come up a little short in the beddy-bye department of late, and it's left me edgy. Besides, I've always felt that breakfast-, lunch- and dinner-meetings are perhaps the least effective way of getting anything accomplished."

Helen Tosco fired another evil-eye salvo my direction, and added in a voice that went with it like ham with eggs, *"Mister* Nebraska, *do* you have any idea who you're talking to?"

"'Whom,' honey, and it isn't you." I said it, as usual, without thinking, and then it was too late to do much except apologize, for what it was worth. I opened my mouth, but Gunnelli spoke first.

"Helen, our guest is one-hundred-percent right. This is a business meeting, not a social call; we should get down to business." Though he said this to her his eyes were on me, as they had been all along. I knew the look. It was the look a cat trains on a potential adversary. He was sizing me up, quite simply. Was I just a smart ass, or did I carry some weight? It was another variation on the old macho could-I-take-him question, only a little more civilized than what goes on on the playgrounds and in the bars. I made my face and the front part of my mind blank. He could take that as candidness or stupidity, I didn't care. There's very little you can lose by having your opponent underestimate you.

To the waiter who stood by, oblivious to all—as is the hallmark of good waiters—Gunnelli said, "Jimmy, you will please serve us immediately." The boy nodded and trudged back to the building, the grass under his feet crushing and crackling like crepe paper.

Again Gunnelli looked at me. "Very well, then, Mr. Nebraska, to the point." He inserted a palsied yellow hand into the inner pocket of his summer suit coat and extracted a smooth-finish leather wallet. From it he selected a single bill, a $1000 note. It was clean and crisp and new-looking, though I knew it couldn't be new: they quit making them years ago. Gunnelli placed it, facing me, on the mesh tabletop and weighted it with a spoon. It was only the second time in my life I'd seen one—the thousand bucks, I mean; I've seen lots of spoons. When I was a lad I had a great-uncle who carried a $1000 bill in his wallet always, in case he got somewhere and needed to buy a car.

I pried my eyes from Mr. Lincoln's face and focused on the old man's. "Those Instant Cash cards are really something, aren't they?"

"Consider this a gift," Gunnelli rumbled. "A goodwill gesture. I will be perfectly happy to pay this much for each and every photograph you bring me." He let that sink in, and it did—along with the understanding of what had triggered the little signal in my head the night before, when I was getting rid of Tom Carra. Subliminally, I'd realized I was reading the tea leaves all wrong. Now it came to the front of my mind: It wasn't the cops Manzetti was trying to keep the pictures from, it was Gunnelli. That was fun to know, all right, but it only raised the same old questions.

So far, at least. In this business there's no telling what sort of trivia or intuition might prove valuable later. I filed it away and, trying not to look at the money, said, "Your man Tom's obviously told you everything that took place last night, so you know I wouldn't turn the pictures over to Manzetti. What makes you think I'll turn them over to you?"

"Because I am not a barbarian. I am a businessman. I do not use that in the way the movies do—'I am a legitimate businessman.' We both know the business I am in, but it is a business, or at least it has become so. So I prefer to do things in a businesslike fashion. Unlike Manzetti, I do not expect to gain what I want by torture. What, so far, has Manzetti achieved by his devices?"

"A stack of pictures."

"So he has," Gunnelli wryly allowed, "but in spite of his methods, not because of them. He still lacks the photographs you control. You made him a laughingstock, from what Tom Carra tells me. Not too many living men can claim they made a laughingstock of Alfredo Manzetti. But it is Manzetti's own stupidity that opened him to ridicule, just as it is his own stupidity that brought the matter of this Morris Copel to the attention of the police. We try to avoid that sort of, shall we say, publicity these days. The times have changed, as Manzetti has been unable to appreciate. They have changed in many respects; thirty or forty years ago, a word would have been sufficient to dissipate the event entirely from public awareness. Today it requires my calling in many, many favors to downplay the situation. So Manzetti has been doubly stupid: he has attracted attention to himself, to *us,* and he has put your photographs beyond his reach."

"He didn't put them there," I said disagreeably, for I realized sourly why Oberon had been ordered to shelve the Copel investigation. "*I* put them there. Out of his reach and out of yours, too, I might add."

Gunnelli sipped at his coffee, somehow managing to spill none. I tasted mine. It was excellent. Shows what you can do when you don't start with the $1.98-a-pound generic stuff.

He set down his cup with a rattle against the saucer and said, "The thousand dollars was merely a preliminary offer. I am, of course, open to reasonable counteroffers."

"Which is reasonable of you, but money isn't the point."

The woman took up the pitch. "I'm not sure you understand, Mr. Nebraska. Mr. Gunnelli has offered you a fair bit of money for the negatives Tom Carra believes you possess. Even if you have only a few—even just two or three or four—we are talking about a rather substantial sum of money."

I finally got her figured out. "You aren't by any chance a lawyer, Ms. Tosco, are you?"

"I am an attorney, yes," she said, switching to the term lawyers think dignifies their profession, even though it's usually used incorrectly. "If that has anything to do with it."

"It helps explain why you have trouble following plain English. Money, to repeat, isn't the point. The photographs are non-negotiable. Manzetti's threats couldn't buy them, your money can't buy them. Luxury yachts, real estate, women—all the same. No sale."

The old man sat back in his chair and studied me like a chess board. I drank some more coffee. Finally he spoke. "I don't understand your attitude," he said.

And he was serious. It was sort of a refreshing question. I gave it some genuine consideration. "I don't expect you to understand it, Mr. Gunnelli," I said slowly. "I don't understand it myself, at least not completely. I'm no crusader, no do-gooder. I'm not even a guy just doing his job, really. Maybe I'm only someone who's seen too much slip away—jobs, friends, dreams, a wife. So maybe I have to do whatever I can to preserve something. The girl in the pictures? Her old man, and the sort of things he stands for? An image I carry of me when I cared more strongly about those things, too? I don't know. What I know is that I'm not turning those pictures over to anyone—unless I'm backed into a corner, in which case you can bet I won't be turning them over to anyone you'd like to see have them."

It was quite a moving speech, let me tell you. Made me wish I still had those pictures, just so I could not turn them over to anyone.

We sat in silence a while. I looked out across the immaculate lawn that rolled away from us and ended against eight-foot-tall hedges through which, at intervals, the tall brick wall could be glimpsed. A rabbit appeared under the hedge. He must've had a secret entrance/exit under the wall. He watched us in that curious way rabbits have of watching you while pretending not to. Shortly he tired of it and bounded off—quick as a bunny—diagonally across the velvet blanket. I couldn't see where he thought he was heading, but he spotted a gap in the brush and, without breaking stride, disappeared into it.

As if he'd been waiting for the animal to leave, Gunnelli spoke as soon as it vanished. "I fail to see how you think your gesture will help," he said measuredly, as if each word were precious. "Manzetti has some of the negatives already. He can use them at will, he can use them to destroy utterly that which you feel you must preserve. You cannot stop him."

"Can you?"

The pale eyes narrowed. "That," he said, "is problematical."

"And I'm to believe that if I turn the pictures over to you I'll be taking positive steps toward cutting off Manzetti between the water and the wind? Come on, Mr. Gunnelli, I'm not entirely dense. There's nothing I can do about Manzetti. That's lamentable, but there it is. What I *can* do is not add fuel to the fire. The extent to which everyone seems het up over those negatives—the extent to which no one seems ready to act until he gets his hands on them— is the exact extent to which I'm inclined to keep them hidden away."

Gunnelli nodded. "You are not dense, Mr. Nebraska, anyone can see that. You are, however, a trifle naïve. Is not adding fuel to the fire, as you say, any help to putting out the fire? After the building has burned, will you expect a medal because you can say, no, you did not help extinguish the flames but at least you did not make them any hotter?"

"And turning the pictures over to you will somehow help."

"You may well be surprised."

I laughed. "I certainly would be. How, exactly, does it help to have you instead of Manzetti blackmailing Mallory? I mean, I can see how it'd help *you,* but beyond that I'm afraid the picture gets a little unfocused."

Gunnelli turned silent. He stayed that way for quite a while. The

woman, too, kept her thoughts secreted. Breakfast came: crois-
sants. Fresh honey. Toast. Spinach omelette. More hot, strong coffee. Jimmy arranged our plates and, silently as smoke, went away
again. I waited until Helen Tosco made herself the first to reach for
a croissant, then I helped myself. It was weightless on my tongue,
like eating flavored air. I half-finished my second cup of coffee
before Gunnelli spoke again.

"Mr. Nebraska, here is a simplistic response to your question:
You have met Manzetti and you have met me. Given that we are
two evils, which do you think the lesser?" Helen Tosco began to
speak—to silence him, I think—but it was he who silenced her,
with a look I wish I could muster. He resumed, hardly missing a
beat. "I have been in charge of this territory for over twenty-five
years. Quietly. Invisibly. Civilly, I daresay. You may not like the
fact that I and my people are here—in fact, I am certain you do
not like it, and I cannot hold that against you. But it is a fact that
we are here, just as it is a fact that we are going nowhere. We will
be here, whether I am in charge—or Manzetti."

I swallowed a forkful of eggs. "That's how serious it is—you
or him?"

He said, "Miss Tosco wishes I were less candid, but I see little
point in coyness. Yes, I think that is exactly what it comes down
to: me or Manzetti."

Helen Tosco's eyes were on me. I looked into her face. It was
like trying to read Sanskrit: impossible, at least for me. I turned
back to my plate, finished my food, emptied my cup and filled it
again from the thermal pot. "And exactly how do you thwart your
nemesis?" I asked Gunnelli.

He wiped imaginary crumbs from his chin. "That should be
obvious. I beat him to the punch." Helen breathed heavily but
made no verbal objection to her employer's openness.

"And why will Manzetti wait for you to do this? Why, for that
matter, *has* he waited for you to do this? He has all he needs now,
he's had it for going onto two weeks. Why does he need a complete set?"

The lawyer said, "Mr. Gunnelli—"

He traipsed across her words. "To avoid embarrassment," he

rumbled. "He may take his photographs to the bosses in Chicago, but the burden of proof will still be on him. In order to overthrow me, he must prove that he has accomplished something that I am unfit to do, or something that I let slip through my fingers because I am old and senile." He smiled the skeletal smile. "If I have similar photographs, he has lost. I need not even take them to Chicago first. I need only wait until Chicago asks me about Manzetti's charges, then I produce them and say I have had them in hand for months, waiting for the elections to draw near, waiting for the elections to be over—whatever I choose to say. Waiting, in other words, for the time to be right, for the proper moment to use them. Manzetti is defeated. Worse, he is destroyed. A coup that fails is death to its mastermind. Manzetti knows this. That is why he waits, why he wants *all* the photographs and negatives. He is— what is the expression—sweating bullets, because he knows that waiting not long enough can undo him as effectively as waiting too long."

I plucked the napkin from my lap, wiped my mouth, crumpled and dropped the cloth into my plate. "Sounds perfectly reasonable to me."

"Then you agree to the offer?" Helen Tosco asked in a voice that was equal parts excitement and disbelief.

"Oh no," I said off-handedly. "The pictures are still not for sale. See, as long as Manzetti thinks I *might* turn them over to you people, he can't act—at least, that's what you say. So I can stick to my original plan—keeping the photographs in a cool, dry and very safe place—and be secure in the knowledge that I will not only be not helping Manzetti, I will actually be thwarting him. Isn't that so?" Neither spoke. I shoved back my chair and stood. "Besides, the way I see it, I now have a double-coverage insurance policy. Neither you nor Manzetti is stupid enough to act against me so long as you don't know where the negatives are and in whose lap they might end up if anything out of the ordinary happens to me." There was a drop of coffee left in my cup. The scene seemed to demand I finish it with a flourish, even if my bladder was on the verge of bursting.

"You seem to enjoy the dangerous life, Mr. Nebraska," said

Gunnelli in an expressionless *basso*. "And it seems, for the moment, at least, that I have no choice but to honor your decision."

"It does, doesn't it."

He leaned forward and shakily shoved the $1000 note at me. "Take this."

"Thanks, but I don't take money I don't earn."

"I said it was a gift, but you *have* earned it. If you keep the photographs out of Manzetti's hands, I consider that a service rendered me."

I didn't like that. It made me feel somehow soiled, compromised, uncomfortable. "I'm not doing it or anything for you," I insisted.

"Nevertheless, I appreciate it. This is merely a token of that appreciation. Take it. I insist."

I wavered, decided I could just as easily gamble it away along with Manzetti's money, picked it up, pocketed it. And felt every bit as slimy handling the fresh, crisp bill as I had handling Manzetti's crumpled, crushed notes. Dirty money is dirty money. Judas proved that.

"Thanks for the breakfast," I said sullenly. "Let's do it again real soon. Don't bother to get up," I said to Helen Tosco, who wasn't. "I'll find my way out."

It was a swell exit, spoiled only by the gate at the end of the long curve of the driveway. I had to stop the car, get out, hunt around until I found the brown wood box containing the electric switch, back the car up enough to let the gate swing open, get out again, trigger the switch, run back to the car and drive through fast before the gate closed again automatically.

I hoped no one from the house was watching.

I parked in the shade across **10** from Marcie Bell's duplex. No inspiration hit, no little muses giving me sage pointers on how to break to her the news that her brother had shuffled off—been pushed off—this mortal coil. Probably there's no good way of doing it, so the muses keep their mouths shut. Who can blame them?

So I got out of the car and trudged across the street, up the walk, through the door, up the stairs. I felt rather than heard her trot lightly to the apartment door. Then she was in my arms, or I in hers, her mouth a cool and soft sensation pressed hard against mine.

I had almost forgotten about the night before, her bedroom, her. It came back quickly, however, very quickly. She broke the kiss slowly, lingeringly, then looked at me in a sly, self-satisfied, half-lidded way. "Good morning," I said lamely. I am not good with morning-after scenes—not that I've had many of them, which is maybe why I'm no good at them. I think most men are uncomfortable with them, and I'm not sure why. Probably tied in somehow with the old macho training, in which we're instructed to be miserly with emotional displays, especially sissy emotions like affection. Tied in also is the idea that "real men" don't reveal themselves, not totally—the strong, silent myth—and the exposure of self that accompanies any expression of love, from holding hands to necking to deeper intimacies, runs contrary to the indoctrination. It's all fine when hidden in the soft dark night, but no good in the clear white light of day.

Or something like that.

"You look bushed— My God, what happened to your face?"

I told her I'd bumped into a door, and that if I looked tired I blamed it on her. It seemed to be expected. She smiled and squeezed my hand and invited me in.

In we went, she first, I following. She wore a halter and very brief terry shorts. From behind, as she danced into the apartment, she appeared to be wearing only the shorts, and not much of them at that. Her backside swiveled with the regularity of a metronome. What was that Groucho Marx line? "That reminds me, I've been meaning to get my watch fixed." Words to that effect. I concentrated on her words.

"I was hoping you'd come by. I'm missing my gold necklace, the one that came loose last night." She tossed her dark hair and gave me a twinkling over-the-shoulder look.

"Try under your night table," I said quietly. "It slid off the table when you put it there." I closed her front door behind me and again she wrapped herself around me ferociously, which didn't make what I had to tell her any easier in the telling. She floated out of the room, toward the closed bedroom door. "Make yourself to home. There's coffee if you want it."

I didn't. Quite the opposite, in fact. I used her bathroom, and when I was finished found her in the living room, in direct line of the fan, whose presence in that environment wasn't so much a luxury as a criterion for the continuance of life. Marcie displayed the gold serpentine chain. "You're a good detective," she chirped. "It was right where you said." She turned her back three-quarters to me. I took the hint and sat beside her to fasten the necklace.

"This clasp's in bad shape," I said as I dinked with it. "You're going to lose the thing for good someday."

"I know. I have to get it fixed, but I'm always wearing it. Except when it falls off, of course."

"I think it'd take the jeweler about five minutes to replace." I finally got it hooked, and she turned to give me another kiss. It brought my blood pressure up to a healthy level, which under other circumstances I wouldn't've minded in the slightest. However, circumstances were as they were. I more or less pried us apart. The look on her face was confused, on the way to hurt.

"What is it?" she whispered. "Is it about Eddie? It is, isn't it?"

I nodded. Doctors always get to say things like, "He didn't respond to treatment," or, "He was too far gone." I had no such luxury. I had to come across up front.

"He's dead," I said.

She looked stupid. "Oh God," she breathed with terrible reverence, or something like it. "Oh Eddie, oh God." With a crack the back of her head hit the back of the couch. She seemed to go slack, empty, as if someone had pulled a plug and all the energy in her bones just bled out. There were no tears, just an ancient weariness in her fine voice when she said, "Tell me."

I slouched back into the couch and crossed my ankles on the table. "It's pretty much as I told you last night, only more so. The pictures, the Mob—the whole bit. And Eddie got caught between two warring factions: the homicidal maniac I told you about last night and the head of the Omaha relations of the family. The maniac wanted the photos in order to buy some power with the Chicago bosses and oust the present boss. I found Eddie's body in a garage on the north side after I left here last night. He's been dead all along, Marcie, ever since he disappeared, or just about. He was selling those nude photographs I was telling you about, but he got caught holding out and they killed him."

"Holding out?" The voice was miles away.

"He was supposed to be selling Crazy Al everything he had with the woman in it, but he gave them some prints he wasn't supplying any negatives for."

"Oh God—so they killed him."

"I'm afraid so, yes. I'm sorry, Marcie, I really am. If there's anything I can do . . ." I looked over at her, slumped on her spine, quiet and motionless, staring off at something I couldn't see, something I would never be able to see, something from her long ago that was now forever gone. I could have cried, but it required too much effort.

"I can't believe it," Marcie Bell said. "Eddie. Gone. Just like that." She looked at me. "You know," she said softly, "when I woke up this morning I thought about what you said last night. I still can't believe that Eddie was involved in anything like this—

I can't help but think there's some horrible mistake, mistaken identity, something—but somehow I knew this morning that Eddie was . . . gone. That he'd never be back. Poor Eddie, he never had a chance.''

I asked her what she meant. ''Just that: from the beginning, everything seemed against him somehow, you know? I hate to say this about my own brother, but the simple truth is that Eddie was a loser. I don't mean anything bad by that, just that things never seemed to work out right for him the way they seem to always work out right for some people. Jobs, friends, girls—Eddie just never had much luck, and what he had seemed to be bad.'' Again she fell silent. I was reluctant to disturb it. However . . .

''What makes you think Eddie didn't have anything to do with the pictures? I mean, the police have known about his, um, activities in that line for quite some time. And I spent much of last night with a witness to the transaction; he wasn't at all vague on the point.''

Her mouth went tight and the muscles in her neck stiffened. ''I don't care about any of them. I knew my brother better than them, better than anyone. I know he couldn't be involved in any pornography, certainly not any blackmail. Where would he even meet such an important man's daughter? Much less photograph her in the nude. No, I *know* it's a mistake, a horrible, tragic, ghastly mistake. Period.'' She unwound from the couch with energy born of anger. ''I know it's early, but I'm for a drink. You?''

She had to ask twice; I was lost in thought. A drink would just about bag me, but I accepted. Noble Nebraska, buckling to peer pressure. I stared into the revolving fan blades as she went into the kitchenette and poured a couple of respectable measures of Jack Daniel's over ice. She brought the glasses into the hot living room, handed me one, reclaimed her place on the couch. ''Well,'' she sighed, ''here's to Eddie.'' She downed most of her bourbon.

I sipped at mine. ''What do you plan to do, Marcie?''

''What do you mean? There's nothing to do. I can't very well call up this Crazy Al Manzetti or whatever his name is and ask him to deliver the body to the Forbush Funeral Home, can I?''

"No," I said quietly, "you can't. And you wouldn't want to. I saw the body and it wasn't very pretty anymore. Besides, after last night's thrill-packed adventure, I wouldn't be surprised if they've already taken steps toward . . . disposal."

"So there you go," she said with finality. "What's there to do? I'll go by Eddie's place and pick up his stuff—Lord knows there's not much—and, well, I guess that'll be the end of it."

That didn't set too well with me. There's something in us, drummed into our heads from the beginning of socialization, from the beginning, perhaps, of the species, that doesn't easily allow us to simply forget our dead. In battle, we risk our necks to retrieve fallen comrades. Rescue workers strive to reclaim victims from hopeless disasters in mines, fires, lakes. And when the dead cannot be reached and loaded into caissons, our sensibilities still demand a tribute for them—a few words spoken over water, a memorial dedicated to the anonymous slain. But no such ceremony for Eddie Bell. *I'll go by Eddie's place and pick up his stuff, and that'll be the end of it.* Indeed yes. Small impact on the world made by such people. Hundreds—thousands, probably—vanish every year, and they are so marginal, so far below our consciousness, that they are literally never missed. Except, perhaps, for a "Whatever happened to that Eddie—what was his name? Beal? Something like that." "Guess he just drifted along." "Guess he must of."

No, that didn't rest easy in me, all the more so because it seemed so easy for Marcie. My news hadn't really affected her— surprised her, yes; saddened, perhaps; affected, no. It wasn't shock; shock I've seen before and she wasn't suffering from it. It simply wasn't that important to her. Eddie was gone; too bad, that's it. I was reminded of when we first met, Marcie and I, the day before, when the little sensors flashed in my head. *Calculating.* That's what had come to mind. Still fit. In fact, it fit even better now. As much as I liked Marcie—or thought I could if I came to know her—as much as I was strongly attracted to her physically, sexually, I still saw in her a powerful and perhaps even dangerous selfishness. Or self-preservation; who can make the distinction? In bed she was as loving and giving as any partner I've ever had; subconsciously, however, you always knew that the giving was only in proportion to what she received. That isn't love. The real Marcie Bell was imbedded, enshrouded, deep within herself, so deep that no one—maybe not even Marcie—could touch her or affect her. It was a hard thing to tell myself, for without too much effort, I knew, I could fall for her. Perhaps for that very reason, then, it was a good thing to remind myself.

Marcie finished off her drink and headed for the kitchen while asking if I wanted another. I hadn't even taken a second hit off mine yet. I declined. She cracked an ice-cube tray in the kitchen and I said, "What about the police?"

Liquor gurgled over the cubes. "What about them? You think I should swear out a complaint against the Mafia? No thanks, friend. I try not to go looking for trouble."

"You just read me a highly impassioned defense of your brother. The evidence is stacked against you, but maybe if we told the police what we know they'd poke into it more aggressively or more accurately than they've been. Maybe they'd find out you're right after all, maybe clear Eddie's name." Or maybe Sal the Gun would just bring more pressure to bear on Oberon's bosses.

She came back into the living room and stood looking out the windows over my head. "With who? Who knows about it? Me? I already know the truth. You? You'll think whatever you want to think anyhow, I know that much about you. The Mafia? Who cares about them? No, I'm for just forgetting about it. I can't bring Eddie back, I can't undo what's been done. I can only keep going." She looked away from the treetops standing perfectly motionless in the stillness beyond the windows. She looked down at me. "What about you, Nebraska, you gonna screw me up?"

I sampled a little more bourbon and set down the glass. "If you mean am I going to run to the nearest pay phone and call the cops, no. There's still a client confidentiality operating here, I think. I don't necessarily approve of your position. But I'll abide by it."

She smiled gently. "Thanks. I knew I could count on you."

"Yeah, I'm a pretty wonderful sort of guy." I stood up. "Well, I'd better be toddling off now. I'm sure you've got things to do, that you don't need company at a time like this."

"Don't I owe you some money?"

It was a hell of a thing to worry about now, but completely in character. "Actually, I probably owe you some. I was only on the job a day, and your retainer'll likely more than cover my mileage, too. I'll work it out and let you know."

"Do. In the meantime, as long as you're still working for me—" The halter was gone in one fluid motion. Instinctively, almost involuntarily, I cupped her breasts, pressed my mouth against hers. I was sure hell with the women all of a sudden. She pushed me back onto the couch.

I woke when she rose. We were in her bed, which we'd moved to in the course of things. She tried to slip quietly from the mattress but the springs gave her away, so I watched her move naked from the bed to the door, admiring the play of lithe muscles under her smooth, perfect, taut skin. She was short but well-proportioned, with the illusion of legginess. As she reached the door I said, "Going somewhere?"

She jumped. "Don't you ever do that to me again." She half-turned toward me. "Yes, I'm going somewhere. To work. I have to pay my private-eye bills."

Leering, I said, "We could probably work out an easy-payment plan, my dear . . ." She stuck her tongue out at me and headed for the bathroom.

A minute later the shower roared. I rose and pulled on my pants and was in the kitchen drinking her cold coffee when she emerged, her hair wrapped in a towel, naked but for droplets of water that dotted her skin where she'd carelessly dried herself. I poured her a cup and asked where she worked. She gave me the name of a trendy bar in the Old Market. "It's a terrific job, too," she said, making a face at the coffee and dumping it into the sink. "They'll probably make me assistant manager this fall." She consulted the clock on the stove. "Unless they fire me for being late today, thanks to you. Can I be there by four? Gotta make the attitude-adjustment hour."

It was a quarter past three. "If you go like that." I licked a water drop from her hip.

"Animal," she said lightly. She moved toward the bedroom. I followed.

"You know, under the circumstances they'd probably understand if you called in and took the day off."

She shook her head and the towel started to unravel. She let it. "I'd rather keep busy. It's better for me. Here I'd brood; there I'm doing something, and something I like. The only problem is the place stinks. I mean really stinks, when it gets hot and muggy like this." I could believe it. The Old Market is just that—the old city market, disused for many years until someone with bucks developed it into all sorts of stylish shops and restaurants and expensive lofts, hang-outs for artistes and collegiates, latter-day hippies and the gay community. It's all beautiful brick and wood—which over the years soaked up and stored every imaginable odor of fish, fowl, vegetable and human being, which it redistributes whenever the mercury climbs and there's no breeze to help cart it away.

I watched her dress in a blitzkrieg of flying clothes. Panty hose. Bra. Striped sailorish top. Dark blue skirt slit halfway up the leg. Rainbow sandals with high heels. Matching rainbow belt. She painted her mouth with a kind of pencil, not a lipstick, applied a little color to her eyelids and ran a brush through her hair. Ten minutes and she looked like a million. I said as much.

"Thank you, sir, flattery will get you somewhere. If you'd like to know where, just come by when I get off work. Play your cards right and I might even let you run a cool bath for me."

"Okay, you talked me into it. What time do you get off?"

She smiled wickedly. "About half an hour after you show up, I bet." I rolled my eyes and she pretended to get serious. "The bar closes at one; I'm usually home within half an hour, forty-five minutes."

"You'll be back by two, then?"

"Perfect."

She finished her preparations, I threw on the rest of my clothes and we left the house together. I sat in my car and with a mixture of sadness and affection watched her drive off. She was beautiful, and she had touched in me something I thought was gone, but she had no true emotions, at least not of the giving variety. She was thus flawed, and that was saddening. It was like meeting a beautiful woman with no mind, or a sailor's vocabulary. A grave disappointment.

But, hell, I was no Prince Valiant either.

And I sat there and thought. Loose ends, too many loose ends. For the second time in as many days, the case was just about ended. Not closed, nothing so satisfying as that; it just seemed to peter out on its own. There was nothing left to do, really, no places left to go. The end, just about. And good riddance. Time to head home and stare at the typewriter. Write. Forget about gangsters and porn merchants and politicians and murderers. Except those on paper. I claimed to be a writer. You don't get there by crashing around after bad guys. Write. Only a couple little errands to perform and it was back to The Book, back to where I could make things work out as I liked, draw events to satisfactory and logical and complete conclusions.

I started the car and drove.

I drove downtown, to the old Professional Building (I know, I know; who'd want an amateur building?) where Mallory's campaign headquarters was located. Only a half-baked notion carried me there. For one thing, it seemed the only base I hadn't touched in the screwy game. For another, I still wondered about the events that had brought Eddie Bell and Al Manzetti to their fatal meeting. If I were Bell and I somehow had the photographs of Adrian Mallory, I would go first to Senator Mallory, to Mallory's people, and demand extortion money. And if I were Mallory or his senior staffers, I would pay the money.

So where did Manzetti come in?

The thought crossed my mind that, since Bell was double-crossing Manzetti, perhaps he double-crossed Mallory as well. Perhaps the plan had been to sell some of the negatives to Mallory, some to Manzetti, and hang onto the rest—those Copel ended up with—for a rainy day.

In any event, I thought Mallory should know what was going on around him, take steps, whatever they may be, to protect himself and his daughter and his political life. It was important to my sentimental as well as political sensibilities. Mallory stood for, had always stood for, a lot of unpopular things, like civil rights and the ERA and educational opportunity and the war on poverty. All the stuff that was passé in the 1980s. Besides, I had been on hand in those ground-floor days when the star began its rise, haltingly, falteringly. I like to think I—or the know-it-all college freshman I was in those days—helped put it there. I hated the thought of it falling, particularly if it fell tarnished. Sentiment is a powerful motivator. It kept me and Jen from taking that final, irrevocable step toward marital dissolution, even if the union was over. It kept Adrian from taking any risks about her predicament, even though they might have saved her. And it propelled me now, even if there was no longer any case.

I put the car in a clammy city ramp and hoofed the two steaming blocks to the Professional Building. Citizens for Mallory was on the ninth floor, in a good-sized space that I think used to belong to a dentist I went to when I was a kid. Most of the room was now given over to a large, bright, noisy bullpen of eight or ten desks. Narrow tables lined the walls; Ma Bell's boys were there, installing phone banks. The place was in relatively good order. When the campaign really got rolling in a couple weeks, though, that would change drastically.

It was a far cry from the olden times. Then we worked out of Mallory's basement—eventually filling it, his garage and a fair percentage of his house. We would've killed for a shoestring budget; ours was more along the lines of dental floss. I was responsible for drafting speeches, writing releases, campaign literature and the like. The drafts I wrote on the backs of left-over handouts a high-school teacher volunteer salvaged. I conned a local priest into donating his parish's mimeograph in an effort to send a "foine" Irish boy to Congress. All of the paid workers—of which there were very few—worked for free for a few weeks in order to help meet the bills. Even so, it looked like we were dead in the water

five weeks before the general election. The money had just about
run out, our chief opposition, the incumbent, was practically printing his handbills on the backs of $10 notes, and it looked like
Mallory would have to throw in the towel for want of cool currency. At the last minute an anonymous benefactor stepped in, just
like in a Frank Capra movie, and gave us an inoculation of cash
that kept us on our feet until November, when, against all odds,
Mallory squeaked in.

Now Mallory was the incumbent, somewhat ironically, campaigning hard against a young, unseasoned opponent who was as
determined to win now as Mallory had been then. Except that neither Mallory nor his hopeful usurper would be hurting for money
this time around.

A sweet young thing for whom the description "perky" had
been expressly invented bounded over like she had springs in her
penny loafers. "Hi!" she chirruped. "Can I help you?"

No witty comeback sprang to mind, so I played it straight. "My
name's Nebraska. I used to work for Dan a lot of years ago, and I
was wondering if he's around this afternoon."

"I haven't seen him today," she said. "He's very busy."
Didn't she think I knew that? "Were you a volunteer?"

"Staff," I said, probably a little testily. "Do you expect him?"

She tossed her head jerkily to one side and looked serious.
"Well, I really don't know. His schedule gets so messed up sometimes."

"Yes, it's a heck of a life, isn't it?" I fully expected him to be
on hand; the actual for-the-money campaigning wouldn't get going
until Labor Day; this was the time for strategy meetings with the
senior staff. "Look, could I at least leave a message? One that it's
very important he get?"

Perky tossed her head to the other shoulder as she said, "Well."
That's as far as she got before a short, fat middle-aged man with a
leonine mane of yellow hair and a malodorous air of self-impor-
tance butted in. "Are you the electrician? Please say you're the
electrician."

"I'm the electrician." Always give the public what it demands.

"Thank God. What are you wasting time here, for, hum? The problem is back here. Follow me." He waddled toward some enclosed offices at the back of the work area. I shrugged for Perky's benefit and trudged along after the fat man. He took me back to one of the four private offices and flung open the door dramatically, gesticulating with flabby arms and sausage fingers, like a high-school declamation contestant. "Look! Just look! How can I work under these conditions?"

It was a legitimate question. The room's central lighting was provided by an overhead fluorescent fixture, one of those two-tube egg crates, standard office issue. For some reason—bad tubes, faulty wiring—the thing wouldn't stay illuminated, no matter how hard it tried. It was a little like working under a flashing neon sign.

"Well, what's the matter with it?" he demanded.

"I think it's broken."

The fat man's lips parted in a little *tch* as he gaped at me. His cheeks were so full that his mouth was thrust forward in a permanent pucker, which he now worked in and out a couple times before sputtering, "Well, of *course* it is! What sort of an idiotic statement *is* that? What sort of electrician *are* you?" The significance of the latter question seemed to sink in. "Wait a minute—where are your tools? Your, your work clothes?" Then he drew himself up to his full five foot five and proclaimed, "You're no electrician!"

"You're telling me. If I were, I'd fix your damn light; it's giving me a headache."

"Then what in tarnation are you doing here?"

I liked that word, *tarnation*. I'd have to work it into The Book. "You invited me back, remember?"

"But—that was because you told me you were an electrician."

"And you asked for that, too." I surveyed the office. Standard steel desk, bookcases crammed with policy titles and looseleaf binders, window with a swell view of the roof of the public library.

His piggy eyes narrowed. "I see," he said levelly. "Very funny. Now what say you get the hell out of here before I call the police, hum?"

I ignored it. "Are you Mr. Schell?"

He raised himself a little on the balls of his feet, which brought him to a towering five five and a half. "I am *Doctor* Schell, yes."

Naturally. It fit his *type*. I've never thought too much of people who insist on the *doctor* prefix unless they're bona fide medical doctors. Come to think of it, I don't like M.D.s insisting on the title either. The designation is a sign of respect, and respect is earned, not automatically conferred upon the completion of so many years of formal schooling. Certainly, it's not something that is insisted upon in any event. But Schell was of that *type*.

Schell added forcefully, or at least more shrilly, "Do I know you? Who are you anyway? How do you know me?"

"My name's Nebraska. I'm a writer. But I used to be a private investigator. That's how I know these things." That, plus the fact that I'd read the nameplate on the desk and decided only FRANK SCHELL would be so passionately interested in getting the lights in the office fixed. But you don't give away all your trade secrets.

"A private eye, hum?" Schell said smarmily. "What are you nosing around here for?"

I tried imitating Gunnelli's silencing stare. I don't think I was too good at it, but I made Fatty blink first. "In the first place, I don't 'nose' around like a pig after truffles. In the second place, if I were nosing around here I wouldn't tell you about it."

Schell tried to reclaim some dignity. "Well, I *am* the senator's chief of staff."

"Terrific, then you should know where he is and when he'll be coming back."

"Well, you must understand, the senator's a very busy man—"

"I understand that. I'm one of the guys who helped him become a senator in the first place. And I know for a fact that when campaigns are gearing up, candidates have been known to frequent their campaign headquarters."

Right on cue, a commotion, a kind of electric buzz, erupted in the bullpen. I stuck my head out the door. It was Mallory, all right, accompanied by a handful of aides, surrounded by a coterie of salivating young campaign volunteers. You'd've thought he was Mick Jagger.

But I could understand the excitement; there was an energy that enveloped him, the aura that seems to surround all people who've dealt with power for any length of time. Real power, that is. Mid-level office politicians, wife-beaters, bureaucrats don't have it. Schell didn't have it, Manzetti didn't. But Gunnelli did, as did Mallory.

And for the female workers—most of whom, to these aging eyes, seemed awfully young—there was the fact that Dan was still a fine-looking man. I had always thought he looked a little like Vic Morrow: tough and sensitive in equal measures. His hair, now slate gray, was receding into a widow's peak, from which he swept it up and back dramatically. He was about my height and powerfully built, his back was a tabletop dressed in a summer suit, his neck a thick mass of sinews, like telephone cables in a thin plastic sheath. A little extra insulation about the middle, perhaps, but still a good-looking fellow. I guessed at his age—fifty-two, fifty-three.

Schell bellied his way past me, puffing across the work area on his stocky little legs, very much caught up in his own importance. Mallory saw him coming, raised his head from a handful of pages he had been given and made ready to say something to the fat man. But instead he saw me in the doorway, let out a whoop and rushed back, past Schell, who watched with pursed lips.

Mallory grabbed me in a bear hug and lifted me off the floor a half-inch, pounded me on the back and arms, called me a son of a gun and—but you get the idea. "God, I haven't seen you in a bear's age," he said fervently. "You heard I was in trouble this time so you came down to help me out, right? Boy, how long's it been, huh? Ten years anyway, I'd say."

"Something like that. Look, Dan, I know you're real busy, but do you have a couple minutes to spare? It's important."

"You bet I do. Come into my office." He steered me toward the door next to Schell's. That worthy, meanwhile, was steaming back toward us. "Senator, we really don't have time—"

"Yes we do," Mallory said sternly. "Have you two met?"

"Yeah, we collided a couple minutes ago," I said.

"Great," Mallory said, pushing me into the office. "You come in, too, Frank, help me get this guy on the payroll again."

We closed ourselves into an office that was a similar, though larger, version of Schell's. More space, fewer books and papers, bigger desk. Office silliness: he who spends the least amount of time at the desk and in the office gets the best and biggest of each. I said to Mallory, "Dan, this is really sort of personal—"

"Hey, anything you can say to me you can say to Frank. If you're between jobs or something, don't worry about it. We'd love to have you back on board, wouldn't we, Frank?"

Frank prudently kept his opinion secret.

I said, "You don't understand, Dan, this is personal with regard to *you.*"

He dropped the pal o' mine routine like an old shoe. "Oh? Then you'd better say it in front of both of us. Frank is my friend as well as my chief of staff and top adviser. If this is important, as you say it is, I want him to hear it."

That wasn't too surprising, and I had no real objection. I didn't like Schell much, didn't like his *type,* but I had no cause to doubt his competence or integrity. Besides, he'd likely find out sooner or later.

"Okay, then." I propped myself on the edge of Mallory's desk. "It has to do with some pictures, and blackmail."

They traded looks. "What sort of pictures?" Schell asked guardedly.

I was glad he spoke; it meant I could look at him and not Mallory when I said, "Pictures of Adrian. The sort of pictures you could blackmail with."

Mallory said brusquely, "Don't let's be coy here, okay? I know you can put words together, man, so do it. Spell it out. What sort of pictures are 'the sort of pictures you could blackmail with'? Is she burning down an orphanage? Running over an old lady? Hanging naked from a chandelier at my opponent's primary victory party?"

"Closer to the latter," I said. I described the pictures.

Schell said to Mallory, sotto voce, "They're the same ones."

Mallory nodded. "Where'd you pick this up?" he asked me. I was thinking of having the story printed on handbills that I could just pass out at this point to save me the effort of reciting it for the umptieth time. I gave them a quick rundown on Copel's visit to my house, how that led me to investigate Bell's disappearance, how that led me to discover that Bell had taken the photos of Adrian. I took it no further than that.

Mallory nodded more forcefully, as if he and I were doctors and I had just confirmed his diagnosis. He clapped me on the shoulder. "Thanks for coming down and telling us this, Nebraska. Hard thing to do, I know, because it is rather—delicate, eh? But I surely do appreciate it, even if we already knew all about it."

"You knew—"

Schell elaborated. "This is the sort of thing you have to put up with in politics, you must know that. Happens all the time, hum? Some kook comes in threatening to blackmail you or some such fool thing."

"This was no idle threat," I said. "He had the real goods."

"We know," said Mallory. "He showed them to us."

"And what did you do?"

"We showed him the door," Schell said with satisfaction. "That's the only way to handle something like this. We booted him right out, told him if he showed his face again we'd have him behind bars so fast it'd make his head swim."

I frowned, feeling very stupid. "But the pictures—were they fakes, phonied up somehow?"

Mallory, who'd been nodding like a toy dog in a car window through Schell's explanation, cleared his throat and looked a little abashed. "No, I'm afraid they were the genuine article. It was my Adrian, I'm sorry to say. In the altogether." We got suddenly quiet and the quiet hung on us like the blankets of humidity that hung on the city. Then Mallory said feistily, as if he had been challenged, "Well, after all, she's entitled to her life. She's a grown woman now. Almost thirty, though she doesn't look it. She can do as she pleases. So maybe she has a boyfriend, and the boyfriend has a camera, and they decide to take a few . . . racy pictures. Maybe you or I wouldn't go in for that"—he tried to look rakish—"or maybe we would. It doesn't matter. When she did it I'm sure hurting me was the furthest thing from her mind. I'm sure they were never intended to go beyond her and her boy-friend's hands. I don't know how this son of a bitch Eddie Bell got a hold of them, and I don't care. As far as I'm concerned, it's Adrian's business, not mine."

It was certainly an enlightened attitude. "Does Adrian know about Bell coming to you? That you know about the pictures?"

He waved his hands like he was clearing smoke. "No, no, of course not. And she never will, either. If I do say so myself, I've become a pretty fair actor since I went to the District, and if I don't want Adrian to know anything out of the ordinary has gone on, she won't know. In fact, I just came back from a long late lunch with her and one of her young friends, and let me tell you, neither of those wonderful girls had the slightest inkling that I had anything on my mind besides what to order." The old boy was facing facts a lot better than his daughter had given him credit for. "Besides," he added, "I *don't* have anything on my mind on that score. It's a dead issue now."

"To a certain extent," I said. "Eddie Bell, at least, is dead. But those pictures are now hot items of interest for the Mafia."

"The *Mafia?*" said Frank Schell incredulously, putting a little laugh into it so it came out "Ma-ha-fia." I never found it a partic-ularly amusing word, but it seemed to provoke risibility in a lot of quarters.

"Okay, 'organized crime' if you're big on euphemism. The point, I think, is that the pictures exist, they are out there, and they can be used against you."

Mallory looked at Schell, whose fat face was as expressionless as a cue ball. One with yellow hair. "Well, yes, I suppose they can," the senator said slowly.

"So what do you intend to do about it?"

Schell said, "We'll do what we do with every crackpot threat: toss them out on their ears, tell them to get permanently lost unless they want more trouble than they ever bargained for."

I was beginning to feel I'd taken a wrong turn and ended up at the broken-record festival. "But these guys aren't crackpots," I said vehemently. "They're for real, and so's their threat."

Mallory put his hands on my shoulders, reassuringly. "Aw, come on, don't you think you're overexaggerating this just a tad? You know, I am a United States senator; I'm not entirely without resources of my own. Let them throw those pictures in my face. I'll tell them what they can do with them, and if they don't follow my suggestion they can be exposed to the cold light of public scrutiny. I have nothing to hide. I have nothing to fear. I have nothing to be ashamed of." I had the feeling Mallory had given too many Independence Day speeches.

"And what about Adrian?" I asked.

"Well—yes, it will be hard, extremely hard on her. Naturally, I hope none of this comes to pass. But if it does—well, it won't be any cakewalk for me either. And as I said, Adrian's an adult. That means she has to learn to take the consequences of her actions. But I'm not worried. I know the hardworking people of this state. I've served them for going on twenty years, state and national. I know what fair-minded, upright people they are. And I know that it will take more than some silly pictures to make up their minds for them." I waited for an "And in conclusion let me say," but it never came.

I looked at Schell. "Well, we certainly can't knuckle under to these bastards," he said, "and we can't do much of anything until—and unless—*they* do anything, hum?"

No, and that's what I hated about the whole damn matter almost from square one: there wasn't a blessed thing in creation to do about any of it, and that's not the way I'm put together.

Not that there was a hell of a lot I could do about it.

"All right, then," I said. "I just thought you should know what you may be up against." I propelled myself off the edge of the desk, trying to console myself with the thought that Manzetti and Gunnelli might stay deadlocked until after the election, when Mallory would either be in a stronger position to fight any threat or would no longer be in office and therefore a much less tempting blackmail target.

Schell made a show of consulting his LCD watch. Mallory seemed not to notice, but I saw that he was firmly, if gently, steering me toward the door, pumping my hand like he expected to get water. "Well, thanks, I mean really. It means a lot to me that you still think enough of the old war-horse that you'd come down here, that you'd be so concerned. It really does. And, look, I'm completely serious about you coming back to work here—hell, come with us when we go back to the District. Christ knows we've got enough work to go around, and the staff almost never has to go without paychecks anymore—isn't that right, Frank?"

"Yessir, senator," said the fat man, who hadn't lowered his wristwatch arm. "Now I'm afraid we are running late for your next appointment . . ."

Mallory let go my hand and slapped me on the back some more. It was a disgusting habit he'd picked up since the old days, a manifestation of the forced bonhomie I suppose you develop when you have to be *on* twenty-four hours a day. I don't know what else I expected, but I was a little miffed that Dan Mallory had become a politician. Still, who of us is as we were ten, twelve years ago?

"Well, there you have it, old son," Mallory was saying. "Hell of a life, eh? You take care of yourself, and thanks again for coming in. Don't be such a stranger, either. And if you change your mind about that job, you just let me know, okay?"

"Sure. Where're you living these days?"

The laugh at least seemed genuine. "God, I'd forgotten your comebacks. I'd like to put you up against some of these right-wing, neo-fascist cretins—"

"Senator, we're very late," Schell interjected.

"All right, already. Thanks again, my friend. Take care. You know the way out. . . ?"

It was the smoothest bum's rush I'd ever seen in my life. I toddled out of the office, picked up some literature and was in the lobby waiting for the elevator when Schell caught up to me. He hemmed and hawed a little, apologized in an extremely half-assed fashion for being such a pompous fool earlier, and finally let me bully him into coming to the point: "Well, I know that you've known the senator for a long time, and that you wouldn't've come down here if you didn't care about him, what he's trying to accomplish in Washington, the projects he's—''

"Criminy, Schell, not you too. I used to crank out that drivel; save it for someone who hasn't heard it. What are you trying to say?"

He took a breath. Saying what he meant, that was a new one on him. "Okay. I need to know—the senator and I need to know—that we can count on your, um, discretion."

I should've been insulted, but I wasn't. "What happened to the cold light of public scrutiny?"

Schell looked embarrassed. "Yes. Well, the senator's a man of high convictions, as you know. He does tend to get a little carried away on them."

"Yeah. Don't worry your head about me. I'm out of it as of about now. But that doesn't mean I'm not concerned for him."

Schell tried to force his mouth into a tight line, but the blubber was too much for him. He looked instead like he'd swallowed a tack, and said, "Don't you worry about Dan Mallory. He's a scrapper. There's nothing he wants more than a good hard fight this time around. He wants to show the right wing a thing or three, and he will, too—you can count on it. He's got the savvy for it, he's got the stomach for it, and that he's down a little in the polls only makes him fight that much harder. No, don't worry about Dan. Nothing's going to keep him from victory in November."

"I have to go now, Frank, my elevator's here. Besides, I already saw *Rocky*." I stepped into the car, but couldn't leave Schell with that look on his face. Just as the doors closed I said, "Don't worry, Frank, you've got my vote."

I'll never know if that's what he wanted to hear.

After sitting in the car in **11** the ramp for ten minutes I finally came to the conclusion there was nowhere to go but home. The case—such as it was—was now definitely over for me. I toyed once more with going back to Adrian, but what could I say? What, that is, that wouldn't just make her life seem bleaker to her than it already did? That Eddie Bell was dead and she'd never have to worry about him again? Sure—and what would I say to her questions about the remaining photographs? That would lead into the Mafia angle, which was an even worse presence than Bell had been. It would also probably necessitate telling her Mallory knew about the pictures—a sentence I wouldn't even get finished before she flung herself in a swan dive off the building.

No, there was nothing I could tell her, nothing that would do anything but make her lot worse for her in her own mind. Now, perhaps, she had at least lulled herself into a false and uneasy sense of security. After all, Eddie Bell had left her alone for a couple of weeks; she could begin to pretend it might be forever. She had no way of knowing how far everything had gone since Bell's disappearance. She might be rudely, brutally, shatteringly snatched from that security of ingorance any day, any hour—but which was worse, having it happen or having to dread it happening, perhaps for weeks, perhaps for months, perhaps forever?

I started the old car and left the cool garage for the harsh, hot streets.

The sky was changing colors, going from a whitish blue to a bluish gray. The overcast was still a ways from evolving into anything that looked like a cloud, but there was a certain texture to it in the west that, with the first feeble suggestion of a breeze from that direction, seemed promising and gave me a certain desolate feeling of expectation.

Magazines, bills and the check I'd been waiting for were in the mailbox. Beer was in the fridge. The landlord had yet to get the busted screens replaced, so the apartment's atmosphere was like a pressure cooker again. I started to open the patio doors anyway, but noticed the winged insects ganging up outside, looking for a place to get in out of the weather that was coming. I flipped on the fan and made a mental note to let someone know his tribute wasn't going to be paid until the screens were fixed. Kick 'em where it counts. Such was my mood.

I drank half a Falstaff, flipped through the mail, got the check ready for deposit. In between long periods of staring off into space.

For some reason I found myself thinking of Oberon. Poor Ben. I wondered if he had any inkling of the real reason for his superiors' making him put Copel's murder on hold, where they and he knew it would be forgotten. Probably he at least suspected it was because a higher authority—namely, Salvatore Gunnelli—was exerting pressure to hush the matter up lest it be traced back to his boy.

Whoa. Wrong—not his boy; his *enemy*, his mortal enemy Manzetti. Wouldn't it have been better to let the investigation proceed, to let OPD trace Copel's murder to Manzetti, to let Chicago see Manzetti's name and picture in the news and know that Manzetti was hardly keeping the low profile they desired? I would have thought that Gunnelli would try to *engineer* something like that, not squelch it. What could he fear from an investigation? That it would link him to Manzetti? If he could see to it that the investigation was canned, he could see to it that the investigation implicated only Manzetti and left himself completely unscathed. Reveal the existence of the photos? That would deprive Gunnelli of the blackmail potential, but he didn't have that card anyhow.

No matter how I looked at it, I couldn't get it to make sense. An investigation into Copel's murder might destroy Manzetti, maybe even Mallory—but wouldn't harm Gunnelli.

Not, at least, so's I could see.

God, I had a headache.

I dragged out my notes and manuscript for The Book and gave
them the once-over, then moved over to my gleaming Smith-Cor-
ona to flesh out the scenes I had sketched earlier. It was tough
going at first. Oftentimes I think the hardest part of writing is
clearing the front part of your head of all the accumulated clutter—
bills and personal problems and what you're missing on TV—and
getting the hell to work. Once you're over that hurdle, it becomes
almost easy. Assuming, of course, you have something to write.
Then later, naturally, you have to do it all backward: bring yourself back up from immersion in the work, forget about the pro-
gression of the story line, the problems and nuisances of trying to
get the story from your head onto the page, and go back to worrying about money and spouses and social obligations.

The last dragged me up out of The Book after almost two hours.
My head still throbbed but it was a remote pain, as if it were
someone else's. I sleepwalked through the place a few minutes—
got a beer, visited the gent's, looked out the window at the graying
day, then dug the phone book out from under the mail.

I set down the beer and looked up the number of the bar Marcie
Bell worked at. She was probably doing marvelously, but etiquette
seemed to demand my show of concern.

A man answered and I asked for Marcie. "She's not in today.
Can I help you?"

A little nonplussed, I explained that I was a friend of hers. He
told me she had had a death in the family or something and so
wasn't coming in today. He suggested I try her at home.

I did exactly that: I got into my car and drove to the other side
of town, to the duplex. It's amazing I got there without killing
anyone or getting killed myself. If you asked me what route I took
to get there, I wouldn't be able to tell you. My mind was totally
unconcerned with such nuisances as traffic safety, was instead
completely occupied with trying to understand the watery, unfocused images that were fast crystallizing in my head, coalescing
like—well, like images on photographic paper. Utterly, inexcusa-
bly criminal to be operating a motor vehicle in that state of mind,
but I got there, somehow.

I barreled through the front door and up the stairs to Marcie's

apartment. The door was locked. No sound came from behind it. I
rang the bell and knocked. Still nothing. I crashed back downstairs
and tried to raise whoever lived in the lower half of the house. No
reply there either. That was fine.

The old red beast was parked at the curb. I went back to it and
got the jack handle from the trunk, wrapped it in a piece of newspaper and strolled nonchalantly back to the house. I didn't need the
crowbar to get into Marcie's apartment; her door gave easily to my
charge card. I carefully locked the door behind me and quickly,
cautiously searched the place, trying to leave no clues but not
really all that concerned. I didn't find anything noteworthy.

After twenty minutes I quit, closed up the place and went down
the stairs. Next to the staircase was a short dead-end corridor that
provided access to the space below the stairs. That space was
walled in, paneled in dark wood that contained one of those hidden
doors like you used to see in people's rec rooms, the kind where
you push on a section of the panel and the door pops back, open.
This particular secret door was betrayed by the presence of a
padlock, a good strong lock that was more than a match for the
jack handle. Unfortunately the hasp through which it passed
wasn't.

The space under the stairs, as I expected, was used as a storage
room, musty, dusty and blacker than a total eclipse. I batted
blindly and found the string to the lightbulb overhead. It was a
dimmer bulb than even I am, but it sufficiently illuminated the
room's few contents: several small boxes crammed into the tapered
end where the stairs met the floor, some suitcases just inside the
door, a bike, and a man-sized wardrobe trunk standing on its right
side under the bulb.

The trunk was roomy enough to hold a pygmy family. It was
also locked, a state that was coming to mean less and less to me.

I broke into it. It contained everything that was conspicuous by
its absence at Eddie Bell's place: the equipment, the chemicals, the
printing paper, the little clock and trays, even the red bulb. I didn't
know much about photography, but it looked to me like everything
you'd need to develop film and print pictures. It would be done in

a bathroom—Marcie's bathroom, Marcie who didn't know of, couldn't conceive of, her brother's pornographic endeavors.

Angrily I went through the half-dozen cardboard drawers in the wardrobe. Scores of photos, many of them the same type as Eddie's shots of Adrian, the photos I had found in Bell's room, the photos I expected to be on the film I had given to Pat Costello to develop.

Adrian appeared in none of these.

Some of the other photos were different. They were instant photos, Polaroids, and they lacked the clothed man who appeared with his back to the camera in all of Eddie's pictures. In these shots only women appeared. Sometimes singly, sometimes with another woman.

Marcie appeared in many of them. She appeared in all of them that featured two women. And six or seven of those starred Marcie and Adrian Mallory.

The sky was the color of gunmetal and an insistent, hot wind now came from the west. I smelled rain on that wind as it pushed the humidity from the atmosphere and sent a shiver through me. On second thought, perhaps it wasn't the wind at all that made me shivery.

I had it in mind that it was now time to have that little talk with Adrian. Not that I had the slightest idea how to begin—or proceed—or wrap up. Somehow she had to be made to realize that her sexual preferences were hardly heinous—hell, lesbian dalliances are the stuff of best-selling novels and made-for-television movies. I knew that Adrian had taken a calculated risk—the risk that someone might recognize her in Bell's photos versus the certainty that her father would learn about her tastes if she didn't agree to pose—and that she couldn't have foreseen the mess that followed. I knew she wanted only to protect her father and her father's opinion of her. But now she would have to be honest with him, and with herself. That would be hard for both of them, but how else could Mallory prepare himself for what he would soon face?

Worse still, I had to make her realize that by making the whole story public she might—just might—be able to save her father. Otherwise . . .

By the time I reached Adrian's I needed the headlights, though it was only a little past eight. I buttoned up the car and fought the wind up to the sand-colored building. I was breathless by the time I got there, the wind literally snatched out of me.

I leaned a little while on the white button next to Adrian's name, with no response, before I noticed that someone had propped open the security door with an old mover's trick: a dime stood on edge in the upper corner above the hinge. The coin bit into the soft wood and was all but buried, leaving the door open only a quarter of an inch or less, but that was plenty. I was grateful enough to be in, but I wondered why people thought they had security doors in the first place.

At Adrian's door I got as much response as I'd had downstairs. Bruised knuckles is all I got as I tried to straddle the line between rousing her if she was in there and rousing the neighbors if she wasn't. As it was, I roused no one. Dejectedly went back down the hall on the thick, quiet carpet. Rang for the elevator. Waited. Looked out the window at the nascent storm. Stepped into the elevator car. Hit the DOOR OPEN button. Went back up the hall to Adrian's.

I rattled the knob. I'd read enough detective novels to know that it's the door the hero spends the most time agonizing over that's the door that isn't locked.

Naturally, it was locked. And bolted from within, no doubt. And chained, too, if she was home and simply not answering the door for whatever legitimate reason she might have.

Nonetheless, I fiddled with it and sprang the knob lock.

And the door opened.

I didn't expect that and I didn't like it either. If nothing else, the dead bolt should've been set, whether Adrian was in or out. Any jerk with a piece of flexible plastic can spring most doorknob locks—I'd just proved that—which is what they make dead bolts for. But I didn't waste time thinking about it in the hallway, waiting to be discovered. I ducked into the apartment and shut the door silently.

Motionless, I waited, listened. Nothing, no sound but the noises that simply exist in a home. Subliminal sounds from elsewhere in the building. The refrigerator. The air conditioning. The pendulum clock in the living room. Outside, the wind.

"Adrian . . ." It echoed back on me. No one home. And yet the hairs on the back of my neck stood at attention while the little alarms in my brain went off like it was a stickup at Fort Knox. I moved through the place, expecting at every instant to encounter its irate tenant. What if she and a friend were taking a little . . . nap in the bedroom? Then I would leave. Quickly.

I breathed again when I reached the bedroom. Empty. The room was a mess—clothes everywhere, bed unmade, drawers half-open and spilling over—but that didn't mean anything; so was my room.

The bathroom was across the hall. As big as my bedroom, too, I noted enviously. I won't even say how big her bedroom was. The bath was designed by someone who had some understanding of what the room was used for: it was actually two small parallel rooms. First you entered a carpeted chamber containing linen closet, vanity with sink and mirrored cabinet, and a full-length three-sided mirror like in a department store. To the left was a door, behind which, I figured, were the toilet and tub. Thus could one member of the family bathe while another shaved in an un-steamed mirror. Positive genius.

I tried the inside door. It was locked. I rapped on it and called Adrian's name. I heard nothing from the other side but the slow, regular drip of water into water. When I turned off the lights in my half of the room and looked under the door, I saw no light from the other side. I put my weight against the door very suddenly and the lock popped easily. The light switch was where you'd expect it to be.

Adrian was in the bathtub and the water was a dark, dark pink, running to red.

I don't know how long it was before I could move. A minute,

perhaps two. Seemed like forever, though, as I stood and looked at her. She was very beautiful and very pale. She looked asleep. Her eyes were closed and the look in her face was restful, even beatific. Entering the room was like entering a shrine.

There was no pulse in her neck. I knew there would be none; the water was too red for that. I reached into it—it was still warm—and lifted one slender arm. She knew what she was doing. The slashes, which started at her wrists where they met the hands, were long and deep and with, not across, the veins. Beyond the sharp pain of a half-dozen razor lacerations, death was painless for her.

If I had talked to her after seeing Mallory . . .

Who could say? I didn't know then and I don't know now what I'd've said to her that would've made anything different. I'll never know.

A brown towel lay near her on the floor. I wiped my hands on it and put it back where it had been, near an almost empty glass. Scotch. Maybe it had helped deaden the pain of the slashes. And the other pain, the one that made the slashes seem less painful by comparison.

I forced myself to look at her again, her naked limbs, white turning to blue, the discolored bath water. There was nothing else to see, because the razor blade was in the other room, on the sink. It was rinsed clean. That's something suicides don't often worry about. Even if they've figured out how to cut their wrists, wash off the blade and hop into a tub six feet away in another room—without spilling a drop of blood in between.

I shut off the lights and left the bathroom.

For the sake of completeness I checked out the kitchen. It looked like a page out of a magazine. A single glass stood in the stainless steel sink. It smelled faintly of bourbon. I didn't touch it.

On my way back to the front door, something glinting in the deep pile carpet caught my eye. I bent over and retrieved it. Then I left, setting the doorknob lock—the only one that could be set from outside without a key—and twisting my hand on it to ruin the fingerprints. Mine and anyone else's.

◇   ◇

The wind continued to rise, though the rain delayed its appearance. The night went prematurely black; no moon, no stars. Branches swayed and whispered harshly at the wind. Panes rattled and whistled in their frames.

I sat in the dark and listened. It seemed to be building to a climax, a crescendo, like a Rossini overture. In the meantime an odd and rather disturbing calm seemed to have settled over me. For no good reason, no good apparent reason, at least. It bothered me a little. Not enough to see what I could do about it, though.

Marcie Bell returned to her place at 9:09. I know, because I was there, in the blackness, waiting.

I heard, above the wind, her car door slam dully. I heard her at the downstairs door. I heard her struggle up the stairs, evidently carrying something large and unwieldy if not terribly heavy. I heard her key scrape metallically in the lock, which conscientious me had reset for her. I heard her enter the apartment. And I heard her gasp a little shriek when she threw the room into light and saw me sitting in the center of the couch. She dropped her burden, a beat-up brown suitcase I recognized as the one in Eddie Bell's closet, and put a hand to her breast dramatically. "My God, what's the matter with you—you get your kicks scaring me to death?"

"Sorry," I said unapologetically.

She shoved the suitcase out of the way with her foot, slammed the door and locked it. "And just what the hell are you doing here anyway?"

"Waiting for you."

"Uh-huh. And how'd you get in here—as if I didn't already know."

"Nobody's a saint, Marcie," I reminded her. I couldn't read the look that came into her eyes. Probably she didn't want me to. At any rate, she abruptly broke eye contact and stormed into the little kitchen, to the phone on the wall.

"You can just tell that to the cops, buddy. I don't think they'll care much for your habit of breaking into anyplace you want to—or for your wit, either."

She lifted the receiver and dialed the first digit.

"Put down the phone." I said it quietly.

She could hear the sound but not the words. It made her step back into the living room, stretching the coiled cord to its limit. "What?"

"I said put down the phone. Or I'll use it to hammer out your teeth."

"You've gone crazy," she said in a kind of awestruck voice. But she cradled the receiver, then came halfway back into the living room, between, I noticed, me and the door. "What's the matter with you?"

"As you say, I've gone crazy, at least a little. That's not so bad. What's worse, I think, is that I'm coming back from it."

She was shaking her head. I wasn't looking at her, but peripherally I could see the motion of her dark head wagging sadly. "You're not even making sense."

I said, "I tried phoning you at work today."

"Is *that* it? Oh, honey . . . I decided not to go in after all. I was halfway there and I got to thinking about what you'd said—you know, about how they'd give me the day off if I asked—and then I realized that I really didn't feel up to it. That I wanted to be alone—which is why I didn't call you—and that I had plenty of things to do, Eddie's stuff to take care of . . ."

"The sum total of Eddie's worldly possessions wouldn't take you more than twenty minutes to assemble and cart away."

"Well, I didn't approach it like a timed test. You know, the place was kind of a mess; I straightened up a little, did the dishes, packed them—that kind of thing. Organized what precious little he had."

"That's still hardly five hours' worth."

Her eyes congealed into shiny bits of ebony. "I had some other things to do, too, all right? Some shopping. Some thinking. Mostly I just wanted some time to be alone."

"Alone with Adrian Mallory."

She frowned. "Is that a name that's supposed to mean something to me?"

"Unless you're having severe short-term memory problems.

You were at her apartment on Seventy-second Street today, sometime between, oh, four-thirty and six-thirty, seven.''

"I don't know any Adrian—Mallory?—and I don't know what
you're talking about, but I resent your questions and your attitude
and your being here. And I'd appreciate it if you'd just get out—
now.''

Instead I produced the shiny artifact I'd snatched from Adrian's
carpet on my way out. Marcie's eye caught it, the way a cat
catches something moving quickly, and her hand went to her
throat, where no necklace rested.

"I told you to get the clasp fixed," I said.

She stared at the serpentine chain as if it were in fact a snake.
The gold cross rotated slowly and deflected light rays from the
room's only lamp.

"It took me a while to get a handle on it," I admitted while she
stared. "Too long a while, which only goes to show that I've been
out of the game too long and probably never should have been in
it, at least not this kind of deadly game. I had little glimmers, little
fitful stirrings, but I didn't even begin to awaken until this afternoon." *And only through sheer dumb chance,* I could have added,
but why spoil the myth that detectives solve everything through
pure sterling reasoning, when in fact ninety-nine percent of "detective" work consists of little more than bumbling around until
you trip over something valuable?

"Even then, I was none too swift on the uptake. I still couldn't
figure how to connect a senator's daughter to a two-bit por-
nographer like Eddie Bell. That came later.''

I expected another impassioned defense of the brother, but none
was forthcoming. The blood did go out of her face until she was
white, though not as white as Adrian in her bathtub. She stood
there dumbly, as if I'd struck her between the eyes with a club.
Her arms hung loose at her sides, which made me think of Alice
the Goon from the Popeye cartoons. Most people are always doing
something with their arms—folding them, putting their hands on
their hips, fiddling with their hair. Something. But Marcie just
stood, as if she'd forgotten about her arms.

Then I became aware of a low moaning in the room, a sound I originally took to be a change in the pitch of the howling wind but which was in fact coming from Marcie, whose face now reddened and twisted into a tearful pattern, though no tears came, just that eerie, unsettling moan. It ended, finally, on a little sigh of air. "I never wanted to see her hurt," Marcie whined in a voice laced with anguish. "I never wanted to see her cry. I loved her."

I waited. Sooner or later the story would come. And it did: Adrian and Marcie had met a few months earlier; I didn't quite catch how or where but it didn't seem an important enough point to ask after it. They became friends, as will happen, and started doing things together—going out for a drink, taking in a flick. Eventually, but, Marcie seemed to believe, inevitably the relationship "heightened," to use her word. They became lovers, she and Adrian. It was a new experience for them both, and, naturally, they spent a good deal of time exploring it. "I'm not a lesbian," Marcie told me, "though I did love Adrian dearly. I was just . . . curious, I guess. To see what it'd be like. And it was marvelous, it really was. But I couldn't see it as a way of life, you know? I like men too much—as *you* possibly have noticed." This last was delivered with a heavy-lidded look that I ignored. She went on:

"But Adrian really got into it. I mean, she jumped in headfirst and never came up for air. She wanted to do everything, try everything at least once. It was as if," Marcie said with a bittersweet nostalgic smile, "she was making up for lost time."

It was a fairly deep thought. If I were a good psychologist or Lew Archer, I probably could've made something pithy out of it. I'm no psychologist, though, and I'm certainly not Archer. I couldn't make anything out of it except to wonder if Adrian was not in fact compensating for lost time, for years lost looking for something, some kind of love, some kind of caring she felt she had missed. Dan Mallory loved her, I knew, but perhaps it wasn't enough, or the right kind. I'd never know the answer to that one, either. But I hoped very hard that maybe she found a little of it, that maybe for a brief instant she had, or even just thought she had, whatever it was she wanted so badly.

In the same spirit of adventure and experimentation that led them into the affair, the women soon began exploring other possibilities—some of them, Marcie intimated shyly, bordering on the kinky. Nothing too heavy. A little fun with silk scarves. A little role playing. A little photography.

I don't know whose idea it was; Marcie didn't say. Again, unimportant. In any event, they took turns photographing one another, and even rigged an automatic shutter release to get both of them together. The pictures were for their eyes only—in fact, Marcie allowed as how looking at them wasn't anywhere near as thrilling as taking them, or even just the *idea* of taking them. Nevertheless, she kept hers in a dresser drawer, which is where Eddie Bell found them.

By the time she reached this point in the narration, Marcie had begun to aimlessly wander the room. She was nervous, she said, upset, she said, she needed a drink, she said, and floated into the kitchen. I declined when asked. I heard the fridge door, the ice-cube tray, the ice in the glass, the gurgle of liquid over the cubes. She returned to the room, cradling the drink in the palm of one hand. We listened for a while to the wind and the creaking of ice in her glass.

"He was just passing through town, the way he would from time to time," Marcie said tonelessly. Overlaid upon the anguish in her voice was now the weariness that had been there when I told her of Eddie's death. "I was at work; I didn't know that he was here or even that he was coming. He must've been looking for money"—she sighed—"and found the pictures instead."

She looked down at me earnestly. "You couldn't believe before that I didn't know about Eddie's . . . photography. Well, of course I did. I knew he'd done it out in California, too. But—well, after all, he was my brother."

That notwithstanding, no cajoling would sway Eddie from his plan once he saw his opportunity. Despite Marcie's pleading and begging, despite her volunteering to pose for him instead, Eddie approached Adrian and gave her a choice: pose for his pictures or have the shots of her and Marcie become public. It was no choice, really.

Distraught, ashamed, humiliated, Marcie broke off the rela-

tionship. How could she face Adrian knowing what her brother—
her own brother—was forcing her to do, knowing that she, in
some way, was responsible?

But now that Eddie was dead . . .

"I thought that she at least ought to know that she didn't have
anything to fear from him anymore. And, yes, I did want to see
her again—I'd wanted to go over there so many times these past
few weeks, just to be with her, comfort her, tell her how sorry I
was. But I couldn't. I just couldn't. Until today.

"I went by there after I picked up Eddie's things. You're right,
that didn't take but half an hour. There was no answer at Adrian's
door, but I knew that she took pills to sleep, the same ones I take,
and they make you dead to the world." She didn't catch the irony
in her choice of clichés. "I had my own key so I let myself in and
found—found her." She bowed her head and pressed a hand
against her eyes, as if pushing away a headache about to emerge.

"Well," she said in a monotone, "I guess I kind of went into
shock—I mean, first Eddie, now Adrian. I got out of there fast,
got into my car and drove, just drove, for hours. I ended up in
Lincoln somehow. Turned around and came back here. For no
good reason; there just seemed to be no good reason not to, not
anymore."

She found her way to the rattan chair and fairly collapsed into it.
"Now you know," she said on the end of a deep sigh that was
intended to clear all the old dust and memories from her body.
"Now you know why I couldn't tell you everything. . . ."

I nodded slowly. "What did you do when you found out that
Eddie was trying to use the pictures to blackmail Senator Mallory?
When you found out he was selling them to the Mob? Didn't you
try to stop him?"

She looked up sharply. "Well, of *course* I did. My God, I
couldn't very well sit by and watch that happen to Adrian, could I?
I *loved* her."

"Yeah. And what about Copel; where does he come into it?"

Her mouth tightened into a line that seemed to run all the way
down her stiffened throat. "Darling, I don't like being cross-examined," she said brittlely.

"You're not being cross-examined, sweetie-pie," I said as smoothly as I could manage. "That's for lawyers. This is interrogation. How did Morris Copel come into the drama and where did he end up with pictures of Adrian?"

"Well—like I told you, I hired Copel to look for Eddie when Eddie'd been gone for a while. I mean, he was doing some pretty awful things, but he *was* my *brother*."

"Yes, I think we have that part pretty well established already. How did you come up with Copel?"

"As you figured," she said reluctantly, "I wanted someone who wasn't too likely to go to the police when he found Eddie. I knew that'd only mean trouble for Eddie, and Adrian, and everyone."

"Uh-huh, but that still doesn't answer the question: How did you come up with Copel? There's no unlicensed private investigators listing in the Yellow Pages."

Her entire face was hatred rendered in flesh, blood and bone. "A fellow at the bar where I work put me in touch with him. *Okay?*"

The wind seemed to have calmed itself a little, but suddenly it picked up again and rattled a window pane like a snare-drum tattoo. I was turned sideways on the couch, and looked out the picture window, into the night. A couple of long streaks of wetness sat on the glass, but nothing you could call rain yet.

I said, "Have you ever read *The Thin Man* by Dashiell Hammett?" I've long since given up trying to pronounce the first name correctly; I said *Dash*-ul, like everyone else.

She didn't care one way or the other, and her voice was as warm as the inside of a Frigidaire when she answered. "You have got to be the most infuriating man in the world to talk to. No, I haven't read it. So the hell what?"

"No particular reason; I was just reminded of one of my favorite parts, a passage where Nick Charles warns someone about one of the people in the story, a woman. He says that most people get discouraged after you've caught them in the third or fourth straight lie, and fall back on the truth. But not this particular woman. 'She keeps trying and you've got to be careful or you'll find yourself believing her, not because she seems to be telling the truth, but simply because you're tired of disbelieving her.' It's a great scene."

"It sounds just really marvelous," Marcie said venomously. "Does it have to do with anything, or is it just a sidelight?"

"You should never resent having your sphere of knowledge broadened a little, Marcie, especially when it applies to you."

Her eyes and nostrils dilated. "You think I'm lying?" It was a dare.

"Like a rug. I know you are; I knew it this afternoon—but I spent the day talking myself out of it because I was falling for you. Like free fall. Without a chute." I said it ruefully.

Her own voice was guarded, in a teasing sort of way. "What is it that makes you so suspicious?"

"I think my mother dropped me on the head while lifting a bottle cap with her teeth." I waited for a spark of pain to escape out the side of my head, which was beginning to remind me it was still there and still sore. Then I said, "You knew too much, as they say in the detective novels. You asked me how I thought Eddie could even meet such an important man's daughter, much less blackmail her. I didn't know; but I was pretty sure I referred to her only as an important woman, not anyone's daughter. Plus you pulled Manzetti's name out of a hat—I don't remember calling him anything but Crazy Al. Of course, maybe you follow the crime scene . . ."

"Maybe I do."

"It gets better. You told me that you had a key to Adrian's— but if so, and if Adrian was dead when you got there, you'd've used it to lock the dead bolt after you when you left."

"I was upset," she said, spitting each syllable.

"Funny, then, that you remembered to set the knob lock—the only one that can be locked without a key if you're on the outside."

Her face was hard and white, as if molded of plaster of Paris. "Isn't that what they call circumstantial evidence?"

"It all is, pretty much. If you want the hard stuff, though, try this: I *knew* you were lying when you told me you loved Adrian. You didn't. I know, because you have to be able to feel in order to love. And because I saw the look in your face and recognized it." I brought out the photos I'd lifted that afternoon, fanned them on the cushion next to me, selected one in which Marcie's face could be seen, and held it up like the winning card. *"This* look. The same look I saw in your face this afternoon when we screwed." I couldn't say "made love" or any other polite euphemism, not now. "The look certainly isn't love, and it isn't even passion or lust or good clean fun. It's a downright businesslike look, because that's what sex is to you. Work. A means to an end. Not an end in itself. You use it for very specific, very clinical, very precise reasons. To throw me off the trail, to blackmail girls into posing for the little porno pics you and your brother hawked around town, to set up Adrian's old man. Goal-oriented sex. You didn't invent it, but you're damn good at it. I think it's real trade paperback bestseller material, Marcie. And the best part of it is, it works." I tapped the pictures on the couch with the one I held in my fingers. "Here's the proof."

She had hunched her shoulders, lowering her head in an animalistic defense gesture, but continued to regard me with hateful eyes. "You son of a bitch," she rasped, and it gave me enough warning to be ready when she launched herself, nails-first, at me. I'd been ripped by those claws already, with no anger behind it. I wasn't about to sit still and see how it felt when she was trying to inflict real damage. I moved to the right quickly, genuflecting in front of the couch, barking my shin on the coffee table. She landed where I'd been sitting and twisted around to scratch at me. I went to grab her wrists but I was too slow. She batted my right arm out of the way with enough force to numb it to the elbow, then took a couple runners of skin out of my throat. It hurt like holy hell, so I let her have it, hard, across the jaw.

She dropped like a bird shot from the sky. For a moment I was scared. But her eyes flickered and she moaned and reached for her jaw, and I knew I hadn't killed her. Which I half-regretted.

I grabbed her by the shoulders and yanked her backward into a sitting position while she whined about it and tested her chin. "I think you broke my jaw," she moaned.

"If you're telling me about it, I didn't," I said unsympathetically. "And since I didn't, we're going to take advantage of the opportunity to do some talking—some straight talking, understand?" I squeezed her shoulders for emphasis. She moaned some more, complained I was hurting her, which I told her was nothing compared to what I'd do if I didn't like the course of our conversation. She dropped her head in what I took as surrender.

"Fine," I said tightly. "Now let's take it again from the top, all right?" Her head bobbed a little, and she began to speak.

It was pretty much as I'd guessed. Marcie and Eddie were in the business together and had been all along. Marcie was the brains—I knew that had to be because Eddie's actions, especially his last, fatal stunt, proved him to be too stupid to find his own ass with both hands. It was Marcie's job to find the girls. This was surprisingly easy; the world, to hear her tell it, is full of young women who are "curious" (Marcie's word) about women, eager to have just one fling with a knowledgeable one. "They're not bi," Marcie said. "They all have boyfriends, fiancés, even husbands. If the opportunity presents itself, they'll try it—then go back to their men. If the opportunity never presents itself, they'll never go looking for it and they'll never miss it."

Marcie was the opportunity. She would slowly, precisely, initiate then escalate the relationship, carefully orchestrate the proceedings, the introduction of the new techniques, procedures, playthings, leading up to the photography. And then something awful would happen—Marcie's no-good brother would "find" the photographs and decide they meant easy money for him. Despite Marcie's pleading and tearful begging, Eddie would insist the girl in question either pose for pictures, which he would sell in the downtown porn shops, or face the consequences of her parents/boyfriend/husband—whichever was appropriate—seeing the pictures and learning she was a degenerate.

Most of the women capitulated. A few took their chances, not knowing until later, much later, that they'd made the right choice:

Eddie and Marcie weren't interested in blackmail to that extent. If a girl didn't knuckle under, it was too much work for them to take it any further. The hell with her; on to the next pigeon.

The last of which was Adrian. With her it had started like any other game, but somewhere along the line Marcie had made a discovery: Adrian was the daughter of a U.S. senator. That put a whole new complexion on things, one quite different from selling dirty pictures on the sleazy side of town.

"It was a chance to make some real money," Marcie said bitterly. "No more of this nickel-and-dime bullshit." I looked distastefully at her, saw the blue beginnings of a bruise alongside her jaw and felt no remorse at having put it there, but no pleasure either. "I had it all planned out. We wouldn't let her know Eddie knew who she really was. She'd think she was just posing for the pictures for the porn shops. We wouldn't put the squeeze on her, either, because it was her old man who really had the money. So we collected the pictures, and I had Eddie take them down to Mallory himself."

"Who promptly threw Eddie out of his office."

Her eyes came up. "How did you know?"

"Sleuthfulness," I said. "What happened then?"

"Well, we were pretty surprised. I mean, of all the reactions I'd've expected, that was about the bottom of the list. I was sure the old man would pay up to keep those pictures out of the papers, with an election coming up and everything."

I was pretty sure that the danger was not so much in the papers getting the pictures—no reputable paper would print them—as in the opposition having them, but I held my peace and listened. Eddie and, especially, Marcie—who was revealing herself to me as indeed the brains behind the operation—were at a loss as to what to do next. They really lacked the know-how to cause Mallory any significant grief. After all, they figured it would be an easy score and had given no thought to what they'd do to make good their threat if Mallory called their bluff. Which, perhaps, Mallory and Schell had sensed. Neither of them was stupid, and both had grown adept in Washington at sizing up threatening forces. Which left the Bells in the cold, waiting for inspiration to hit, opportunity to come rap-tapping at the door.

They didn't have long to wait. "Two, maybe three, days later Eddie called me up. He was very excited. This fellow Manzetti'd gotten in touch with him. Manzetti said the word was on the street about Eddie and the pictures of Mallory's kid. The problem was, Manzetti said, that Mallory knew that someone like Eddie, working alone, couldn't possibly hurt him. He didn't have the clout or the connections. But Manzetti, being with the Mafia . . ." She shrugged the end of the sentence. "Well, Eddie met with this Crazy Al, who seemed okay, you know? And by then I figured the whole thing was working out to be more trouble than it was worth—and I wasn't too keen on us being involved in anything big enough to have the Mob interested. So I told Eddie to get the best price he could out of Manzetti and unload the pictures on him. We'd wash our hands of it then."

"And you'd wash your hands of Eddie, too."

"What're you talking about?"

I grabbed her shoulders again and rattled her brains a little. "Cut it out, sister. You set Eddie up, you held back some of the negatives but left in the prints, knowing they'd check, knowing they'd kill Eddie and you wouldn't have to split the money with anybody."

She yanked her shoulders from my grip with a couple sharp jerks of her torso. "Of course I wouldn't, 'cause there wouldn't be any money, just like there wasn't any money—because they killed Eddie. Wise up, idiot, this isn't one of your detective books. I didn't set up Eddie. I couldn't've gotten anything that way. Holding back the pictures must've been his big idea. He never thought we should play it straight with Manzetti. Eddie had this bright idea that since Manzetti didn't know how many pictures we had, we could keep back a few, maybe for another buyer, maybe to make a little extra on the side.

"I told him to forget it, that that was the sort of bright idea people ended up in cement overshoes for, that we weren't going to find any other buyer after the Mafia got their hands on the pictures—once the word was out, no one'd go near them. I thought I had Eddie convinced. I guess not. I guess he tried to hold back a few for himself; it would be just like him to carefully hold back the negatives and forget all about the prints." She slumped forward again and covered her eyes with a hand. "Poor dumb sucker. He never had a chance, he just never really had a chance."

We'd already done this scene once before today, but I let her alone with her thoughts. Perhaps five minutes passed before she spoke again. "What else do you want to know?"

I asked again about Copel. He was a guy, just a guy that Eddie'd met somewhere, somewhere among the sorts of places guys like Eddie meet guys like Copel. Marcie hadn't met him, of course—Marcie didn't meet people like that, that was Eddie's job, that and to keep Marcie's existence a secret. Marcie may have loved Eddie, as she insisted, but she saw to it from the start that it was Eddie, not Marcie, who would take the fall when the fall had to be taken.

But when Eddie had been missing for nearly two weeks, it became necessary for Marcie to emerge, at least partly. She continued the fiction of the maligned but still loyal sister—the bit she pulled with me—told Copel that Eddie had mentioned him to her once or twice, asked if he'd seen anything of Eddie the past week or so. Copel hadn't, of course; Marcie hadn't expected him to. She'd expected him to volunteer, for a fee, to look for Eddie, and Copel didn't disappoint. He took the case, took the key to Eddie's room and took off. Marcie never saw him again.

The rest, as they say, is history.

I figured already that Copel had found the withheld photos of Adrian in Eddie's apartment, recognized the woman and the potential in them, and pocketed them. He would've already heard on the grapevine that Crazy Al killed Eddie, and put two and two together. His next step was to try and sell his newfound photos to Manzetti—whose mania put an end to that and all of Copel's other little schemes.

The ice in Marcie's glass had melted. She drank the bourbony water and asked in a voice that was fatigued, defeated, lifeless, if

that was all, if I would please leave and let her alone, let her sleep.
It wasn't quite all.

"Why did you go to Adrian this afternoon?"

"I . . . I don't know. . . ."

So I grabbed her by the upper arms and tossed her into the
couch. Tough guy. I also wrestle bunnies, barehanded. "Then
make something up," I snapped, "but make it good."

"All *right*," she wailed. "With everything, I thought I'd at
least tell her that Eddie was dead, okay? Put her mind at ease a
little. She wasn't anything to me, she wasn't worth anything to me
anymore, but there was no point in letting her spend the rest of her
life worrying."

"Aren't you good?" I came up off the couch and crossed the
room.

"Where're you going?" Marcie wanted to know, and her voice
suddenly lost the weariness it had held.

"I wanted to get busy on your Nobel Prize nomination," I said
and picked up the scarred brown suitcase.

"You put that down," she said threateningly. But impotently,
and we both knew it.

I opened the case. It still held the camera case, as well as the
jeans and shirt that had been in Bell's closet. I picked up the camera case, unzipped it.

Right on top was the crumpled brown envelope that Morris
Copel had given me the night before last, before he died in my
living room. And inside were the strips of negatives I'd given to
Adrian Mallory the following morning.

Marcie Bell had grown very quiet. I put down the camera case
and the suitcase and waved the envelope at her in true Perry Mason
style. "This is what you went after, isn't it? When I told you how
Eddie died, you knew what he'd done, and when you didn't find
the pictures at Eddie's today you knew that left only two possibilities: Copel took them or I did. And either way, the odds were
good that I had them—unless I'd done something stupid like give
them to Adrian. If I gave them to her, you knew you could weasel
them out of her—you knew she was crazy about you. And if I

hadn't, then you figured you'd eventually weasel them out of me, because I was getting to be pretty crazy about you myself.

"But Adrian was the softer touch, so you started there. And you told her about Eddie's death. And you told her why he was dead, all about Manzetti, and maybe you even let her know how it was all going to fall apart for her father on account of the Mob. But probably she figured that part out for herself. Just as she figured she'd fucked it all up for good—everything: her life, her father's life, his career, you name it."

I threw the envelope at her. She flinched, but it came nowhere near her. "Whose idea was it to cash it in, Marcie? Did Adrian come up with that herself, or did you plant the notion in her anguished brain? Did you two sit around the apartment, her getting sloshed on Scotch while you nursed along a bourbon, and discuss the various merits and demerits of assorted suicide methods? Which of you decided on the blade? Which of you ran the bath? Which of you held the razor and opened the veins?" My voice had grown too loud for the small room; I realized it when Marcie's voice came and was barely a whisper.

"She killed herself. I was with her, I held her when she did it, I steadied her hand and I waited until she was gone—but she killed herself."

"Fine distinction," I muttered.

Marcie tilted her head back, eyes closed, mouth drawn half open. "What happens now? The police?"

What indeed? My civic responsibility was clear; hand her over to the law and let justice weave its tortuous if not torturous course. Which is an attractive proposition only if you have a fairly solid belief in the correlation of law and justice, which I do not, not all the time. Frankly, I couldn't see what good any of it—or anything, for that matter—would do at this point. So I lowered my voice and tried to sound like Robert Mitchum. "No police," I said, "if you play ball. I don't want to see you again, ever, under any circumstances, and the best way you can ensure that is to blow on out of this burg and never come back. Got it?"

She didn't budge.

"*Got* it?"

Languidly she lowered her bruised chin and raised her eye-lashes. "Yeah, I got it. And if I leave you'll keep the police off my back?"

"No guarantees, lady. They won't get your name from me, but whatever they come up with on their own they come up with on their own."

She nodded slowly, smiled in a superior, self-satisfied, defiant way, and said, "You know I'd probably walk out of a courtroom."

"Maybe you would," I allowed. "But then again, who knows. And even if you did walk, you might have to hang around behind bars a hell of a long time before you did. That is, if the Mob let it get that far. But it's your neck, punkin, your choice."

"You damn son of a bitch. I'll go."

12

Little remained to be done. I left Marcie Bell's apartment quickly, as if I couldn't leave quickly enough, and entered the windy world. Down these breezy streets a man must go. I paused at the door of my car and looked up. It seemed even later than it was, on account of the skies having darkened so early. Now they were even darker, half-hidden by black, smoky clouds. The wind, strong as ever, still carried the scent of rain, but continued to hold out on the promise.

I got in the car and went around the block to the Paradise Lounge. It's one of those cool, dark bars that hasn't anything going for it except it's a bar. There's no floor show, unless you count the color television; no entertainment, unless you count the jukebox and small square of linoleum, much too shiny to have ever had many dancers use it. Of course, the place was nearly deserted, and the lack of attractions may have been why.

At the rear was a pay phone, and that was attraction enough for me. I rang up Mallory's campaign headquarters. It was late, but they should've been working late, I figured. I figured right; I recognized Frank Schell's voice on the other end.

"Nebraska," I said. "Get me Mallory."

"The senator isn't here," Schell said guardedly. "Perhaps I can help you . . ."

"I doubt it, Slim. But I wouldn't sweat it. If I were you I'd be worrying about whether I could help Mallory. Whether I could save his skin. Not to mention my own."

"I'm . . . not sure I catch your drift," Schell said amiably, and I realized he must've been within others' earshot. "Can you be a little more specific?"

"Can and will. You and Mallory meet me at his daughter's apartment in"—I checked my watch, for no good reason—"half an hour."

"I'm afraid that's impossible. The senator's speaking at a fund-raiser tonight. In fact, he's probably in the middle of his remarks right now."

"In the middle of the last remarks he'll ever make as an office-holder, you mean," I said tightly. "Half an hour." I hung up on any reply.

I gave the machine another quarter and called the Walnut Hill station. It was a longish shot, but Oberon seemed to be on night shift these days. Or had been: a somewhat flustered desk sergeant finally allowed as Oberon wasn't available. I hung up on him, consulted my wristwatch again, then the phone book, figuring Oberon would forgive me the late hour when he heard what I had to tell him. I fished for another coin and phoned his house.

Oberon answered on the second ring. "Yeah."

I identified myself and apologized for calling at an hour when respectable people are asleep, or getting ready to be.

"Skip it," Oberon said curtly. "I was up. What's the problem?"

"No problem. Just the opposite, in fact. I think we can put the kibosh on the whole Copel-Bell-Manzetti thing tonight."

"I told you once already, 'bo, there isn't any Copel-Bell-Manzetti thing anymore."

"Yeah, but this has gone beyond that now, Ben," I said. "It turns out that Bell was involved in a blackmail scheme. On account of it he got involved with Crazy Al, and on account of *that* he got dead. Copel fits in because he tumbled to what Bell was up to and tried to pick up where Bell fell down. With the same results."

Oberon's voice was slow in returning to the wire. When it did, it sounded more tired than it had the day before, in Oberon's office. Worry started gnawing at my guts. Oberon said, "You don't get it, pal, do you? No one cares about Copel or Bell. They're small fry. Too small for our glorious police division to get worked up over."

"That's where you're wrong, Ben. Yes, Bell and Copel are nothing to get bent out of shape over. But they were involved in something big, very big, and something very, very important. That's why you got leaned on to back off the case: someone was worried where you might end up."

"Oh, yeah? And where might I end up." He'd been at the bottle, damn it; I wasn't getting anywhere.

"I'm at a pay phone," I told him, hoping he was sober enough to realize that meant I couldn't talk freely. I gave him Adrian's address and told him to meet me there in a half hour. "We can have this thing wrapped up in forty-five minutes," I assured him.

"Look, pal, take my advice: forget the whole thing. It's not worth the energy to bust your buttons on it and just get slapped down. Or worse."

"Ben, what are you talking about?"

"What I'm talking about is that if the big shots don't want you snooping around in their business, you shouldn't go snooping around in their business. If you're fond of breathing, that is. You yourself said this is big enough that someone put the arm on the division to bench the investigation. You think I didn't know that?

You think that I could spend fifteen years on the force and not know a rat when I smell one? Shit, no. But if it's that big, it's bigger than both of us, buddy. And I don't know about you, but I got a wife and three kids and a mortgage to look out for." There was a long silence. I listened to it, stunned. When Oberon's voice came back it sounded a long, long ways away. "I turned in my badge today," he said simply.

"Ah, Ben . . ."

"I don't know why, either, I mean, I know why—I just don't have the stomach for that kind of bullshit anymore—but I don't know if it's because of them doing it or me being too gutless to do anything about them doing it, you know?"

I knew. "Ben, if we blow the cover off this, they won't be able to touch you. We'll get the goods on anyone involved in the thing. We'll take it to the city commission—hell, the unicameral—make sure it gets on the news—"

Oberon was laughing, but there was no humor in it. "God, you're an optimist, all right. What makes you think you know how far something like this can extend? This is a clean town, at least it has that reputation, but is it only because the dirt's well hidden? Think about it, pal. But do yourself a favor: *just* think about it. Or write it up into a book and send me a copy sometime."

"Ben—"

"Autograph it for me, too, okay?"

"*Ben*—"

The phone went dead in my hand. I cradled the receiver and rested my head on the wall beside the square, squat phone. A woman's name and number were scratched into the fake wood paneling. I felt like calling her up and asking if I could come over. I certainly didn't want to have to go to Adrian's. I didn't want to see what she looked like by now. I didn't want to have to think about it anymore. I wanted to go home and go to bed and wake up somewhere else, someone else, someone who had never been in this line of work and never would be. Too much was happening, too much was turning to dust and collapsing when I touched it. Too much.

Somebody had fed the jukebox. A song whose words I didn't know but whose tune was hauntingly familiar all the same reverberated mildly in the dark and followed me out onto the street. The song was about people moving into and out of each other's lives, about saying hello and saying goodbye, saying goodbye to Hollywood. . . .

This sure as hell wasn't Hollywood, but I could certainly relate to the sentiment.

People with more sense than me were staying off the streets. The WOW announcer said tornadoes had been sighted in the area, but none officially. Let's hope it rains, he said, because tornadoes can't strike when it's raining. Uh-huh.

For a fat man, Frank Schell could get a move on when properly motivated. I had to sit in the car listening to the radio and the wind for only five or six minutes before I saw him and Mallory, huddled against the elements, hands buried in topcoat pockets, scurry into Adrian's building. I decided to give them some time. I gave them close to ten minutes, then ran to the building. The security door was locked. Mallory must've had a key, which they used to get in. I didn't; I tried the buzzer. Again I recognized Schell's voice, even over the tinny speaker, even as shaken as it was.

"Ye-ess?"

"Nebraska. Let me in."

"I don't—"

"There should be another button on the speaker box. Hit it."

He must've found it, for the door buzzed and I ducked through it. Schell waited at the elevators on Adrian's floor. His moon face, previously a bright shade of pink, was now the color of soiled linen. His yellow hair looked sweat-dirty, lifeless. His fingers were in constant nervous motion, like animated bratwurst. "She's dead," he blurted before I got off the lift. "Adrian. Nebraska, she killed herself."

"No kidding." I went past and let him dog-trot after me up the hallway. The door to Adrian's apartment was open five or six inches. I went in, took a quick inventory of the kitchen and living room, and found Mallory where I'd expected him to be: next to his daughter.

Dan Mallory sat on the carpeted floor next to the tub, his back against the toilet, his eyes looking at nothing on the opposite wall. His right arm was drenched to the elbow. The hand was underwater, holding one of Adrian's hands. The water was a lot darker than it had been before, and Adrian was a lot paler, bluish and . . . bloated. I tried not to look at her.

It was harder to look at Mallory. He'd turned old since that afternoon, nothing like the man I'd watched stride triumphantly, confidently, into his campaign headquarters that day. The skin of his face was curiously nerveless, slack, boneless. His forehead was coated with a patina of sweat, but that may have been because he still wore his topcoat.

"She's gone," he said, and it was the sound of anguish. "Gone." He looked at me, through me. "And you knew it, too, you son of a bitch. Didn't you? You set this up so I'd come and find her . . . find her . . . like this." The bleary eyes spilled over. "You wanted me to see her like this, didn't you, you motherfucker? *Didn't you?*"

I looked from Mallory to the corpse to Schell, whose eyes were locked on the body the way a kid will be glued to a monster movie on the tube. I looked back. She no longer was beautiful. She no longer looked peaceful. She looked horrible. She looked—dead.

"You better believe it," I said to Mallory with such sudden, unexpected vehemence that I felt my muscles tighten and jerk. "I wanted you to see it just as it is, the slashes, the bloody water, everything. Not in the antiseptic surroundings of the morgue. Here. Where she died. Where you killed her."

"You bastard!" he yelled and, with a splash of red water, started to scramble to his feet, no doubt to punch me in the nose. But he wasn't very agile and managed only an ungainly crouch before I shoved him back against the toilet, which he tripped over and then sat down on, hard. He was lucky the lid was down. "You bastard," he repeated. "You can't talk to me that way. I'm a United States senator—"

"For the time being. And I *can* get away with it, because it's true. You killed her. You killed her just as surely as if you'd stood here and opened her veins for her.''

Mallory sat on the can, bunched over as if he was going to launch himself off it and butt me in the belly, panting heavily as if exerting himself. His eyes were locked predatorily on me. Not accusingly: hatefully.

I said, "Do you have any idea how much I admired you, how much everyone admired you? Your integrity, your humanity, your vision. The decency with which you seemed to conduct your life. It went beyond all that Camelot crap back then. Yes, you went to Washington during those times, as a part of all that, but you transcended it. You carried the torch, the ideal, after Camelot disappeared. And you illustrated how it could be, how it ought to be.

"Except that it was a lie, all of it, at the root.''

I turned to Schell. "It was you who got me to thinking. This afternoon. You told me not to worry about Adrian and the pictures and the election. You told me Mallory wouldn't let anything stand in his way. That wasn't the half of it. Mallory never let anything stand in his way.'' I went back to Mallory, who hadn't budged. "Back in that first campaign you wouldn't let the lack of money stand in your way. You were sunk, but you wouldn't let that stop you.''

"We found the money,'' Mallory said. "You were there, you remember. A large donation . . .''

"*Anonymous* donation. And how well-timed! It never occurred to me to question it, to wonder who the money came from, why he'd stayed in the background until it was almost too late, and how he happened to come forward when he did.''

Mallory was silent, but his eyes gave a whole series of lectures, with slides, that said nothing good about me.

"Sal Gunnelli was our anonymous benefactor, Dan, wasn't he?'' I said softly, wishing to hell Oberon was there to hear this. "When you knew you were losing for want of cash you went to him and you cut a deal with him. He'd provide the cash, you'd provide the senate seat. Shit, for all I know he rigged the damn election. Here I've been running around the past couple days thinking the Mob was out to buy itself a senator, never dreaming they've had one for the last twenty years.''

Mallory's face tried to match the color of the bath water, and nearly succeeded. "You son of a bitch," he snarled from a face suddenly gone ugly. "You bastard, you'll never be able to prove these baseless innuendoes.''

"I don't want to. I don't have to. *I* know, and that's enough. I know you're bought and paid for, have been all along. No wonder you threw Eddie Bell out without a second thought; you knew that one call to Gunnelli and Bell would end up on the bottom of a river someplace, explaining to the fishies how he got there. And so it would've gone, too, except neither you nor Gunnelli could know that Manzetti would see this as his chance to discredit the boss and rake in all the chips. And he knew how to do it: He'd get the pictures from Bell—the entire collection, else the whole thing could blow up in his face later if any stray photos surfaced—and take them to Chicago to illustrate that Gunnelli was too old, had lost control, that even a second-rate loser like Bell could touch one of their most valuable pieces of property—that's you, Dan—and would've, too, if he, Manzetti, hadn't stepped in and saved the day by skillfully taking the photographs and the photographer out of the picture. So to speak.

"It's lucky for you and Gunnelli that Manzetti wasn't so terribly skillful at being skillful. Else it would've been all over before now. Incidentally, it *is* all over now.''

"You're ranting," Mallory sneered.

That I was, but it didn't make me wrong. In fact, I knew I wasn't. I finally had all the variables, or all the significant ones, had values assigned to them, had them arranged in the proper order, and had used them to reach a quotient. It was the only possible sum, the only way everything made sense—why Manzetti and Gunnelli were each so hot for the pictures but willing to settle for a dim assurance that I wouldn't turn them over to the other; why Gunnelli had bought off the cops to halt the Copel investigation before it could uncover the photographs, the Mob connection and the fact that Mallory already belonged to the Mob; why Mallory hadn't the slightest fear in the face of the very real threat to his career that Bell posed.

I found myself looking at the senator. A better man than I would've felt some sympathy, some compassion for him. I felt little more than hatred and loathing. No sadness—surprising, not to feel even a small twinge when one of your golden idols turns out to be made of dross. Maybe the sadness would come later. Now there was only the cold blue flame of hatred.

Mallory's attention had wandered from me and back to Adrian—not, I think, the Adrian who lay disfigured and dead in our midst, but the little girl he had known in life. He said, to no one, "She was so beautiful. I don't understand why this happened . . ."

"Yes you do," I said cruelly. "And that's the problem. You understand too well, because you killed her and you know it." It was the second time that night I'd used the line, but it was equally true both times—and it certainly grabbed people's attention. Mallory's head snapped around and trained on me like a guided missile. He said nothing. I said, "It took you eighteen years—from the day you made your devil's pact with Gunnelli—but, by God, you got it done, Dan." I nodded toward the corpse. "And a bang-up job you did, too."

Mallory knotted and reknotted his fists, squeezing the blood from them until they were the color of bone. "How can you say that, you bastard," he growled. "I did everything for her, and when I couldn't I at least saw to it that it got done. You should know that better than anybody—why do you think I asked you to look out for her back then? Because I couldn't do it myself, you stupid— You filthy son of a *bitch*," he sobbed raggedly, pounding his chest in his fury, "I did everything, everything for her, everything I could, everything anyone could've done in my position—"

"Yeah, your *position*, Senator. God, you still don't get it, do you? You sacrificed everything—mainly Adrian—to Gunnelli, to your own thirst for—for—I don't know. Power—money—*position*." My heart pounded alarmingly inside me and I felt light-headed, wavery, suddenly removed from the scene. Tremulously, I sucked a breath. It tasted of blood and death and something gone putrid. "You killed her, all right," I mumbled thickly through numb lips. "Killed her all those years ago. Took her this long to die is all."

He looked as if he was about to jump up and break me with his bare hands like a broomstick. I half hoped he'd try, because I figured I could take him and I'd've loved the excuse. I forced my mouth to work. "Well, look at the bright side: at least she doesn't have to be around to see her old man revealed as the hypocrite he's always been." He didn't rise to the bait. Too bad; I had no more stomach for trying to goad him into motion. I turned to leave.

And I found myself looking into the wrong end of a shiny automatic I'd've never guessed Frank Schell carried.

"Son of a bitch," I breathed.

"Just don't move," Schell said nervously. I just didn't move. There's nothing worse than a nervous man behind a gun; all the crime novels tell you that. "I don't want to have to use this thing, but I will if you make me," said the fat man. "I can't let you destroy this man and his career, all the fine things he's done for his state and his country. The best interests of his constituents, that's always been foremost in his mind. His record shows that." The fat man's voice turned earnest now, and there was a pleading, persuasive look in his sweaty, pudgy face. "The work, that's the important thing. Sure, we've had to make some compromises along the way in order to get things done. That's politics. But we never compromised the work, never, and that's what's important. The work that we've started—just *started*—can't be thrown out, not like this. You must understand that, Nebraska, you were there at the beginning."

I said I understood it. I also said I didn't see what Schell thought he could do about it. "You can kill me," I said, though I wasn't sure it was a good idea to remind him, "but that won't change anything. It just means that everything will start to unravel for a different reason. Everything else will come out, though, sooner or later. In any event, Frank, it's all over."

"*No*. It isn't. Not yet. It's a long damn ways from being over."

He turned to Mallory, who had sat silently, motionlessly, through the testimonial. I might have been able to get the gun from my hip pocket before Schell could react. He probably wasn't that expert with firearms. But neither was I. I played it cool, and cursed Ben Oberon for sitting at home nursing his hurt feelings and a bottle while I did his work for him.

"Senator, grab his arms," Schell was saying. "Use the belt from your coat and tie his arms behind his back."

Mallory started, as if awakened from a dream or a trance. "What—what are you doing?"

"Trying to save both our necks," Schell said reasonably, as if talking to a child. "If we do this carefully, it can look like double suicide. Nebraska's prints will be on the blade. We can say he and Adrian used to be lovers, but Adrian had ended the affair—" He stopped suddenly. He was helped to stop by the unmistakable, unyielding pressure of a gun barrel on his back, dead center between the kidneys.

"Save the speeches for the voters, Baby Huey," a deep voice cooed in his ear. Schell's face went slack and ashen, his piggy eyes bulging in the sacks of blubber that surrounded them. He dropped his gun without it being suggested to him.

"You certainly made me sweat it out, you sadistic bastard," I said hotly.

"This is gratitude?" Ben Oberon complained.

Epilogue

Adrian Mallory's suicide gave Senator Mallory's campaign a shot in the arm: the sympathy vote. Straw polls that showed him at best neck and neck with his opponent now put him eighteen, twenty points ahead. Mallory carried on with tragic courage for about a week after Adrian was buried; then it was abruptly announced that he was quitting the race and retiring from public life. No one knew why. Almost no one. Mallory knew, and Schell; I knew, and Oberon. And Gunnelli knew. Mallory's retirement was the price I exacted from him in exchange for the pictures I had—now had for real—of Adrian. The party scrambled for a good replacement, but it was too late; the opposition walked away with it in November.

Before the election rolled around, Alfredo Manzetti was found in George's Car Barn with his head half sawed off by a garrote. OPD took Tom Carra in for questioning, but nothing could be made to stick. It was written off as an intramural vendetta, and we all forgot about it inside of a month.

Gunnelli retained control of his territory, thanks to the pictures I gave him to counter Manzetti's takeover attempt. It was, as Gunnelli himself had said, the lesser of two evils, and the course that Ben Oberon and I decided on that night in Adrian Mallory's apartment. That and the end of Mallory's political career. Gunnelli agreed to it. He lost his senator but he kept his kingdom and his power. Six weeks later he was dead. A blood clot broke off in one of his "old pegs" one night and went straight to his heart. They found him in bed the next morning, cold as a snowman.

A week or so after Adrian died I drove by Marcie Bell's house. A vacancy sign was in the yard. I went up and inquired about the place, as if interested in renting the apartment. In the course of things I asked about the previous tenant. The landlady—who occupied the lower half of the house—said she thought the young woman had moved to Arizona or New Mexico or someplace like that. For her health, she thought.

I finished The Book early that fall and after a little work found a daring publisher. It appeared the following spring to some kind reviews, made a little money, made a little more money in paperback, was optioned by a producer you've never heard of for a film that never got made, and sank gracefully from view.

Jenny showed up on the doorstep Christmas Eve with a bottle of Krug and two suitcases. She stayed through New Year's. Later I got a card from her in St. Thomas.

I couldn't talk Ben Oberon out of his decision to leave OPD; neither could the commission, though they gave him a medal in the attempt. He became the chief of police in a little Minneapolis suburb, where he sails a lot and from which he sends a card every Christmas.

And I made good on my promise to blow the dirty money pressed on me by Manzetti and Gunnelli. Thirteen hundred big ones. I found a bookie and put the whole bundle on an equestrian nose, a million-to-one long shot, a fleabag whose next stop was the glue factory. The bookie thought I was a loon, but what did he care. He went along with it.

And wouldn't you know it—the damn nag won.